Almond Scones and Accusations

THE FERNWOOD MYSTERIES
BOOK ONE

ASHLEY SAMUELS

TCA PUBLISHING

One

S tupid phone and its stupid updates.

The overnight update had turned off my alarm. I'd awakened ten minutes after I normally left the house for work. Almost a full *hour* after I typically got up.

I glanced at the clock on the wall as I dashed through the kitchen on the way to the garage and winced. "Oh, I'm so late." I huffed and continued toward the door.

My cat, Millicent, let out a soft meow as I skirted past where she sat on the white quartz island.

I skidded to a halt, backing up several steps to scratch her behind the ears. "Sorry, Millie." Leaning in, I pressed a quick kiss to the top of her fuzzy head. "I can't give you all the loving you want this morning. I'm late!" With one last smooch, I hurried away, snagging the tote bag containing my life from the barstool.

Keys jingling, I ran out the front door of my little white cottage, only to stutter to a halt again so I could go back and lock the door.

"Come on, Laney. Get it together," I muttered, turning the key in the lock.

Task done, I spun around and sprinted for my bright blue

SUV parked at the curb. The locks beeped as I hit the button on the fob. Yanking open the door, I flung my tote across the center console onto the passenger seat. My foot was on the brake and I was hitting the start button as I settled in.

Buckling up, I pulled away from the curb.

Slow down, Delaney. You won't do anyone any good if you're dead. My mother's voice floated through my mind. It was something she'd said to me more than once in my thirty years on this planet. I had a tendency to go full tilt and damn the consequences.

Adjusting my grip on the steering wheel, I forced myself not to speed—much—as I left my neighborhood and hopped onto the main road. So I'd make a few less cookies today. Big deal.

I blew out a breath, trying to keep my eyes off the clock. It'd be a *lot* fewer cookies…

Ten minutes after I left my house, I pulled up to the church my family faithfully attended every Sunday. I struck a deal with the pastor to rent the commercial kitchen several days a week for a small fee and a selection of baked goods on Sundays for the congregation. Eventually, the goal was to own my own bakery and expand into a line of breads and bagels, in addition to the sweets and custom cakes I did now. I still made a few of the more savory items but mostly stuck to the sweet stuff. For now, though, this arrangement was a win-win for everyone.

Getting out of my vehicle, I jogged through the parking lot toward the building. Even in my hurried state, I took a moment to soak up the beautiful sight of the sun rising between the mountains, bathing the small white church in a golden glow. I couldn't imagine living anywhere else. The big cities had their perks, but there was nowhere like Fernwood.

With the sun on my face, my mind calmed a little more. The to-do list still unfurled inside my brain, a hundred miles long, but it felt more conquerable now. Keys in hand, I headed for the double doors beside the stairs leading to the church's front entrance. The kitchen and event space were in the basement.

I let myself inside and flipped on the lights as I descended the carpeted concrete steps. In the kitchen area, I set my tote on the counter against the wall.

Time to get to work.

"But I need music." Holding up a finger, I spun around, locating the radio on top of the fridge. I turned it on and an upbeat country song about someone's boots filled the room.

Humming along, I washed my hands and got to work.

It wasn't long before the scent of chocolate and other assorted pastries filled the space. Throughout the morning I worked steadily, making up a little of the time I lost. Luckily, I didn't have a special event today. Just my normal route.

I glanced at the clock.

Which it was time to start.

The last batch of cupcakes had about five minutes left in the oven, which was perfect. I could load up while they finished.

Grabbing my tote, I dug inside for the keys to my dessert truck—Fernwood Flour & Hearth. The church was also kind enough to let me leave it parked in the rear of the overflow lot, making it easy for me to load up.

With my keys in hand, I picked up a stack of hunter-green bakery boxes full of cookies and headed outside. It took me several trips, but I soon had everything loaded into the bakery cases and food warmers inside the truck. A bungee cord or a special latch secured each door—a necessity up here in the mountains, where the roads looked more like giant snakes.

After stashing the last of my dishes in the dishwasher and turning it on, I made sure the ovens were off, locked up the church, then left.

Today, my little bakery truck was headed to the local

outpatient center. It was always a big hit there with staff and patients alike.

It also had the added bonus of being nearby, which was a blessing after the start I'd had to my day. In four minutes, I turned into the parking lot, pulling up behind Tyson Harris's burrito truck.

He leaned out his window, waving, as I got out, tote bag over my shoulder.

"Hey! I was beginning to wonder if you were going to show."

I grinned. "I'm not late. Not yet."

He chuckled, lifting his wrist to point to his watch. "Barely."

I wagged a finger at him, still smiling. "It still counts."

"You're just lucky you don't have to cook anything."

"True." I wouldn't deny that. There wasn't much prep for me. Not on-site, anyway.

Rounding the side of the truck, I unlocked the rear door and stepped up inside. I hung my tote on the hook I'd installed on the wall, then unlatched the windows and pushed them open, locking them into place. Removing all the door latches, I stowed them in the crate under the counter. After booting up the card reader and iPad in my tote bag so I could take card payments and track sales, I was ready for my first customer.

Two

Sweat trickled down the side of my face. I reached for the small fan clipped to the shelf beside my head and angled it more toward me. I really should have sprung for the truck with air-conditioning in the rear.

But no. I'd theorized that I lived in the Cascades. Summer didn't get *that* hot. And when it did, it never lasted long. Plus, it rained a lot here.

I picked up one of my laminated menus and fanned myself. I should have opted for the air.

Movement outside brought me back toward the window. I pasted a smile on my face that turned more genuine when I saw who was standing there. "Hey!"

"Hey, yourself." My older sister, Daphne, stood at the counter, a cheerful smile on her pretty face. Beside her was her boyfriend, Morgan Dean.

"What's up? Did you come to get a cookie fix?"

"Always." Daphne's smile grew. "I'll take a frosted sugar cookie, please."

"Sure." My gaze shifted to Morgan to ask him what he wanted, but Daphne wasn't finished.

"Oh, and one wedding cake." She held up her left hand, flashing me with a diamond ring.

I froze for half a second, then squealed. "What!" Backing up, I turned and scampered for the door and out of the truck.

"Let me see that!" I ordered as I hurried around the corner of the truck. Reaching out, I grabbed my sister's hand and took a closer look at the square-cut diamond solitaire now gracing it. "Oh, I'm so excited for you." With a yank, I pulled her in for a tight hug.

Laughing, Daphne hugged me back. "Thanks, me too."

I eased away. "When did this happen?" My gaze swung between her and Morgan, who stood to the side, smiling at us.

"Last night," Daphne replied. "He took me to that new place on the lake, Schmidt's Seafood, then proposed down by the water after dinner."

"Really? That sounds lovely."

"It was." Daphne turned her head, beaming at her betrothed. "Anyway, we came to share the news, and I was serious about that cake. Will you make it?"

"Of course I will." Ideas were already running through my head. Daphne liked clean lines and rich, bold colors. It wouldn't surprise me at all if she picked royal purple or a deep teal as one of her wedding colors. "We can sit down sometime soon and go over what you want."

"That sounds good. We'd like to get married this fall."

"This fall?" It was already June. That wasn't much time to plan a wedding. "When in the fall?"

"Probably mid-October. I know it's quick, but I've always wanted a fall wedding. I mean, think of the colors!" She gestured to the trees all around. "And I don't want to wait until next year. I'm already thirty-two." She cast a mock scowl at Morgan, like it was his fault she wasn't getting married in her twenties.

I chuckled. "Thirty is not old." I had just hit that milestone, and I didn't feel any agedness creeping up on me.

"Says the woman who just turned thirty last month."

"And with no husband prospects," I reminded her.

"Oh, whatever." Daphne turned a quick glance on Tyson Harris, who leaned through the window on his food truck to hand a burrito to a nurse.

Sinewy muscles rippled in his forearm and a dimple shone in his cheek beneath his wavy dark hair as he smiled.

"He would be your man in a heartbeat." Daphne nodded toward Tyson.

I lifted a shoulder. "Maybe so, but that doesn't mean I'm interested in him."

Daphne rolled her eyes. "I do not know what's wrong with you. He's a catch."

"Maybe," I hummed. The truth was, Tyson didn't make my blood pump. Not the way it should. Sure, he was handsome, but I wanted a man who could make my heart stutter with a look. Tyson was just... a nice guy. "But we're not talking about my love life right now. We're talking about yours. Do Mom and Dad know? And Darcy?"

"Yes. And no. Morgan asked Dad for my hand. I showed Mom my ring this morning. I haven't seen Darcy yet. I figure we'll stop by this evening. I'm hoping she'll agree to be our photographer."

"I don't see why she wouldn't." Our younger sister was an artist of many talents. By day, she taught art at the elementary school. By night, she painted. In her spare time, she took random, amazing pictures. Several of her photos and paintings decorated my house.

Morgan's phone rang. I glanced up in time to catch the deep scowl that took over his face as he looked at the screen. Muttering under his breath, he touched Daphne's shoulder. "I need to take this."

She looked at him, a hint of a worried frown on her face, before turning back to me.

"Everything all right?" I asked.

She waved a hand. "It's fine. Probably just work."

I gave a soft grunt. That was not surprising. As a small-town attorney at the only firm in the area, Morgan spent a lot of time fielding phone calls. "Well, hopefully, it's nothing serious."

Daphne lifted a shoulder. "There's some case he's been working on that's pretty important, I guess. His boss has been riding him kind of hard lately." She scrunched her nose. "I hope he actually gets to eat lunch with me and not at his desk again."

I took another quick glance at him. From the look on his face, I hedged my bet that he'd be sharing his lunch with his desk blotter again. But I didn't want to burst Daphne's bubble, so I pasted a cheery smile on my face. "Hopefully," I said. "How about that cookie now?"

Daphne's expression brightened. "Sure."

Backtracking, I returned to my dessert truck and opened the cupboard where I kept the frosted sugar cookies. Sliding the drawer out and using a set of tongs, I slid one into a paper bag, then opened the chocolate chip drawer. Morgan liked those. I bagged one up, then leaned through the window to hand them to my sister. "Here you go."

"Thanks, Laney." She took the bags, then turned to her fiancé.

He hung up the phone as she took a step toward him, the deep, scowling frown still on his face. "I need to go."

I watched Daphne's shoulders fall.

"All right. Here." She held out the cookie bag. "At least take this with you."

Morgan took the bag and peeked inside. I was pleased to see a bit of his frown ease.

He glanced up. "Thanks, Delaney."

I smiled. "You're welcome. I hope your day gets better."

"Oh, it will." Anger simmered in his dark brown eyes. "Phil's going to get a piece of my mind. I don't care that he's my boss. This is ridiculous. I'm not the only attorney on staff." Leaning down, he dropped a distracted kiss on Daphne's lips. "I'll see you later."

"Okay."

He raised a hand in farewell, making eye contact with me. "Thanks again for the cookie, Delaney."

"You're welcome. And congratulations, again."

"Thanks." Waving once more, he turned and jogged away.

Daphne huffed. "So much for lunch."

"You can eat here with me, if you want." I never minded having my sisters in the truck. I liked the company. Being a solo baker was lonely sometimes.

"Thanks, but I think I'll just get it to go and head back to work."

"You're sure?"

"Yeah. Morgan isn't the only one with work fires to put out."

I smiled. "You're a physical therapist. What kind of work fires do you have? Other than cranky patients, I mean."

Daphne chuckled. "They're enough. But actually, I have a personal improvement plan to go over today for one of the therapy assistants. She's been coming in late a lot and messing up patient files." She rolled her eyes. "I know I'm supposed to say I love those plans and they're highly effective, but they're not. At least not that I've ever seen. People have to want to change, and our local health system doesn't pay employees on her level enough to make them want to." She backed up. "I'll call you later. We'll set up a time to talk about what I want for my cake."

"Sounds good. I already have some ideas. I'll sketch them out to show you." That would keep me occupied this evening while I vegged out on my couch, watching classic reruns.

"That works. See ya." Turning away, she waved.

I waved back, watching her walk off.

Cake ideas swirled through my brain. I let out a happy squeal. This was exciting! I'd figured it was coming. Daphne and Morgan were nearly inseparable outside of work. They'd been that way from the beginning of their relationship.

My fingers itched to grab a notepad and a pencil and start sketching. But I didn't want to get interrupted. The next group of staff from the outpatient center would be coming out any moment for lunch. Once I was in the zone, I preferred to stay there. It made me grouchy when I had to stop before I was ready.

So, I busied myself tidying up my truck and refilling the baskets where I kept bags. I was putting the box with the extra sacks away when the fresh wave of customers arrived.

Smiling to myself, I stepped over to the window. Despite the way the day started, things were looking up.

Three

"Oh, come on, sweetie. Just a couple more miles. We're almost there!" I patted my dessert truck's gray dashboard as the engine sputtered and the entire vehicle shimmied as I tried to pull away from the stop sign at the intersection of Amherst and Roland. It began acting up the moment I started it when it was time to leave my second job of the day. Dinner at the food truck rally in the park. The engine had chugged several more times than normal before it turned over.

I hadn't really thought much of it. Just that it was a little weird. But I figured maybe the battery was beginning to fail. I'd owned the truck a couple of years and had never replaced it. This shimmy and the stalling, though... That wasn't a failing battery.

The truck jerked again as the engine's pistons skipped. It sputtered a few more times, then settled into a soft knocking noise for several seconds before completely giving out.

"No, no, no, no." I turned the key, cranking the engine. It whirred, but didn't catch. "Come on, baby. We're almost back." I tried again.

Once more, it just whirred and refused to start.

Letting out a frustrated growl, I slumped forward, resting my forehead on my hands. I didn't want to call a tow truck. It would eat up most of my profits today to get the truck towed to the garage and looked at.

But I didn't really have a choice. It couldn't stay parked in the middle of the road.

Sitting back, I put the vehicle in park and turned the flashers on, then reached for my tote to get my phone. Pens clacked together as I rummaged around on the bottom, trying to find the small, smooth rectangle.

Finally, my fingers closed around it. Taking it out, I woke up the screen.

"Crap." My shoulders sagged in defeat. I didn't have a signal. "Because why would I? Freaking mountains..." Grasping the door handle, I climbed out and walked to the edge of the road, holding my phone in the air.

The signal bars stubbornly refused to light up.

I probably needed to hike to a higher elevation. Of course, I'd broken down in a small valley between two peaks.

Silently, I cursed my decision-making. I'd taken the back way to the church to avoid the construction on the highway. It took about the same time as going through the mayhem, but it was a lot less frustrating.

Until now, anyway.

Blowing out a breath that ruffled my blonde bangs, I walked up the hill away from the truck. Around the bend, the valley opened up a bit. Maybe I'd get lucky and could call from there.

The sound of a car engine reached my ears. Hope lit my chest. Maybe they'd have a better signal.

Lowering my phone, I turned, trying to pinpoint the sound. It was coming down the hill. Ahead of me. I broke into a jog, hugging the mountain. I didn't want to get hit when whoever it was came around the bend.

My legs burned as I ran up the road's steep incline. I spent entirely too much time in the kitchen and not enough on my treadmill. "Oh, dude, if you stop, I'll give you all the free desserts you want." I did not want to hike out of here.

Getting closer to the bend, I slowed. It might be a better idea to stay here on the straightaway. The driver might not see me when they came around the bend if I was too close to the corner. They'd be focused on the road.

The engine noise grew louder.

A frown creased my forehead. That didn't sound right. It should be getting quieter. They needed to slow for the curve.

No sooner did that thought cross my mind than a car whizzed past the bend. It didn't stop, didn't even slow, and missed the curve.

A bang rent the air, vibrating my chest. The screech of metal shearing swiftly followed. I winced at the sound and watched in horror as the car careened off the roadway and down the side of the mountain into the trees.

"Oh my gosh," I breathed. I could scarcely believe what I'd just witnessed. It was like watching a movie scene. Accidents like that just didn't happen in real life.

Feet rooted to the pavement, I stared at the spot where the car disappeared. The trees swayed and softer bangs echoed through the forest as the car rolled downhill.

Finally, it registered that I'd just witnessed a horrific car crash and needed to help the occupants. Adrenaline surged in my veins, setting me into motion.

The rubber soles of my athletic shoes slapped the asphalt as I ran toward the gap in the guardrail. I skidded to a halt next to the twisted metal and looked over the edge. Here, the mountain slope descended several hundred feet before it leveled out into a gully that ran parallel to the road. A silver SUV stood on its nose at the bottom.

"Oh, geez." There was no way I was getting down there without help.

I lifted my phone, praying for a signal.

I had a bar!

"Please work," I whispered as I dialed 9-1-1. I put the phone on speaker, not wanting to risk moving it from its current spot. Even the few inches to my ear could be enough to disrupt the phone signal up here.

I held my breath as I waited for the call to connect.

Ringing erupted from the phone.

"Yes! Oh, thank the Lord."

"Emergency dispatch, do you need police, fire, or medical?" A woman's voice came over the line, and my shoulders sagged in relief.

"Um, probably all three. I'm on Amherst Road just past Roland, heading into town. There's been an accident. A car went through the guardrail and over the side."

"Okay. Is anyone injured?"

"Probably. I can't tell, though. The car is on its nose at the bottom of the gully."

"Did you see how many people were in the car before it went over?"

"No." I didn't even see the driver, it had all happened so fast.

"Is it just one car?"

"Yes. They missed the curve."

"All right. I've got help coming. Can you tell me your name, please?"

"Delaney Fowler."

"Thank you. Please stay on the scene, Ms. Fowler. The police will want you to give a statement."

I snorted. "Not a problem. My truck broke down, so I'm stuck here until I can get a tow."

"I'm sorry to hear that. A truck will probably arrive soon after the emergency services. It sounds like police and fire will need a hand to retrieve the car. You can talk to the tow truck driver about towing your vehicle as well."

"Definitely. Okay, thank you."

"Yep. Can you get to the car without causing harm to yourself?"

I peered over the road's edge again. "Probably not." I looked again. "Maybe. I'm not sure. Definitely not while I'm on the phone." It was too steep to only have one hand free while I climbed down.

"Okay. Only try if it's safe. I need to take another call, but please call us back if you have any additional information."

"I will, thanks." I bade the dispatcher goodbye and hung up.

Heaving a long breath, I pocketed my phone. Edging closer to the ruined railing, I peered into the ravine again. Man, that was a long way down.

"Hello?" I called.

No answer.

I cupped my hands around my mouth to amplify the sound of my voice. "If you can hear me, I called for help!"

Again, I listened for a response, but only the soft rustle of leaves and the chirp of the birds reached my ears.

I clenched my fists, pulling my lower lip between my teeth and worrying it.

What if someone was really hurt? Like, bleeding and would die from blood loss before the ambulance arrived, kind of bleeding. It could be close to ten minutes before help arrived.

What if there were children in the car?

I peered down the embankment again.

The slope wasn't *that* steep. And there were plenty of trees and other things for me to hang on to.

I let out a soft huff. "Oh, you know you're going down there, Delaney, so just get on with it."

Squaring my shoulders, I picked my way past the tattered guardrail.

My foot slid, and I let out a quick shriek. Arms windmilling, I reached for a tree branch. The bark bit into my palm, but I stayed upright.

"Whoo, boy. That was close." Taking a deep breath, I willed my heart to slow, then took another step, more carefully this time.

I slid several more times on my way down, but having learned my lesson with the first slip, I made sure to keep one hand attached to something when I moved my feet. It only took me a couple of minutes to safely reach the spot where the trees and some boulders finally stopped the car's descent.

"Hello!" Hanging onto a tree limb just twenty feet from the car, I tried to peer through the windows on the smashed silver Mercedes SUV. The angle was wrong, though, and the splintered rear window was tinted. I couldn't see the driver, or anyone else inside, for that matter. The smoke drifting out from the underside didn't help, either.

Planting my foot, I let go of the tree I held onto, then side-stepped my way to the back of the car. Loose dirt, pine needles and small bits of rock slid beneath my shoes, skittering down ahead of me. I dipped into an awkward lunge, extending my left leg to stop the slide as I came up to the driver's door. The vehicle rocked slightly as I used it for balance, but the trees it was wedged against kept it from tipping further.

"Hello?" I grasped the door frame and straightened, pushing the curtain airbag aside.

A man about fifty years old sat in the driver's seat, slumped forward, the seat belt keeping him from resting against the steering wheel. A quick glance around the rest of the interior revealed it was empty.

"Sir? Hey." I reached through the broken window and nudged the driver's shoulder.

His head wobbled and a drop of blood rolled off the end of his nose to land on the dash.

"Sir? Can you talk to me?" I nudged him again, harder, but he still didn't respond.

Turning my hand, I pressed two fingers to his neck.

Nothing.

Moving them around, I searched for a pulse for several seconds, but there was nothing. Not even a flutter.

Above, the sound of tires squealing on the bend drew my attention. I glanced up through the broken trees, fully expecting another car to come crashing down. My muscles tensed as I prepared to run away.

But nothing happened.

I blew out a breath. Someone must have seen the broken guardrail and panicked.

I glanced up again, then frowned. Was that a person standing up there?

Stepping away from the car, I waved. "Hello!" I needed help. I couldn't do CPR on the man until I got him out of the car, and I wasn't sure I could do that on my own.

The shadow above shifted, then disappeared.

"Hello?" I called again. Were they going to call for help?

I heard the distant thud of a car door closing. A moment later, the soft whir of an engine accelerating followed it.

"Did they just drive away?" Glaring up the hillside, I huffed, then spun around. "Fine. I guess I'll do it myself."

But how?

I eyed the mangled driver's door. It would be a miracle if it opened. The entire front end of the vehicle was smashed into some boulders. We were near the bottom of the gully but not all the way down, which was a good thing. A stream ran through here, and the water would have made this so much more difficult. As it was, I didn't know how to get into the car. Everything was bent. The impact had pushed the engine and passenger compartments together, bending the car's frame like an accordion.

I had to try, though. Smoke flowed from the undercarriage. It was only a matter of time before flames erupted.

Grasping the window frame, I held on tight and leaned back, yanking on the door. A small gap opened.

"Yes! Okay. This might be possible." Propping a foot on the rear passenger door, I used it as leverage and yanked again.

Sirens echoed distantly through the forest.

Oh, thank goodness. Help was coming.

I yanked on the door again, widening the gap to about six inches. I needed a lot more to get the man through.

Metal bit into my palms. One hand slipped off, and my fingernails caught on the frame, ripping one.

"Ouch!"

Shaking my hand, I muttered a soft curse under my breath, then repositioned my grip and tried again.

The sirens grew louder. So did the gap in the door.

"Come… on!" I pulled several times in rapid succession, but I simply needed more leverage. Smoke swirled around me, stinging my eyes and making my throat tickle.

I turned and put my butt against the car, lifting a foot and wedging it into the gap. Shaking my hair out of my face, I blew the few wisps that remained away, then braced myself.

My leg muscles shook with the strain. Metal groaned. So did I.

Sucking in a breath of smoky air, I tried again. The door held on for several seconds, then suddenly it gave way. I lurched forward, my foot slipping off, and stumbled a few steps before catching myself.

"Oh!" I spun around and hurried back to the car, batting the airbags out of the way to get to the man. "Sir! Hang on. I've got you." I leaned in, coughing now, to reach around him in search of the seat belt buckle. My fingers fluttered over it, and I pushed. With a soft click, it released.

The man slumped forward.

"Oof!" With the tension gone on the belt, gravity weighed on him, pinning my arm between him and the steering column. "Crap." Huffing, I wiggled, working my hand under his arm. Grabbing hold of his opposite sleeve with my free hand, I backed up.

He tipped sideways, a complete dead weight.

"Oh. Oh, geez. You're a heavy sucker, aren't you?" Readjusting my grip, I bear-hugged him and pulled.

He slid free, but the weight of him threw me off balance, and I fell back, landing hard on my butt.

"Ow." A rock bit into my butt cheek, and I winced. That was going to leave a mark.

Giving the man a shove, I pushed him off me and onto his back. "Sir?" I got to my knees, hovering over him. Blood covered one side of his face. More coated his chest. I pressed two fingers to his neck, hoping I'd been wrong before.

But there was still nothing. He wasn't breathing, either.

Smoke tickled my nostrils, and I coughed again. We needed to be further away. It wasn't safe to stay here.

Hooking my hands under his arms, I lifted his upper body off the ground and tugged.

He moved just a few inches.

"Oh, come on. You don't weigh"—I tugged harder—"that"—I tugged again—"much!"

He scooted over the ground. I didn't stop, just backed up faster, using the momentum I'd gained to get us away from the smoldering car.

After twenty feet or so, I set him down, then knelt next to him. I checked his pulse again, and when I still felt nothing, I scooted forward.

Blowing out a breath, I linked my hands together. "You can do this, Delaney," I muttered. Placing my hands on the center of his chest, right over the blood stain, I started compressions. His color was terrible, so I didn't hold out much hope this would do any good, but I had to try.

The sirens screamed louder. I sent a quick glance up and saw emergency lights flashing through the treetops. Help had arrived.

I didn't stop, though. All while people amassed at the top of the hillside I kept pumping, singing the Hanson song the first-aid instructor taught us in the class I took several years ago. I'd never heard the song before that class, but she'd been an older millennial, so it was one she knew well. I had to admit, it was the perfect song for this. The timing and beat were right, plus, it was catchy, which made it hard to forget.

I made it all the way through the song and was halfway through a second cycle when the first emergency responders slip-slided their way down the hill.

"Are you all right?" a firefighter called.

"I'm… fine. I… saw the… accident."

The man stopped next to me.

"Delaney?"

I glanced up, still pumping away. Sweat trickled down my forehead, running into my eye. I wiped my face on my shirt and looked at him again. "Hi, Mark." Mark Kenilworth was an old friend from school. Not that it mattered. I saw him at least once a week when I parked my food truck near the fire station. He always bought himself a chocolate chip cookie, sourdough bread for his wife, and sugar cookies for his two young daughters.

"How long have you been doing that?" He stopped next to me, opening one of the kits he carried to reveal a cardiac monitor. In our town, our firefighters were also paramedics and EMTs.

"Don't know. Six minutes, maybe."

"Can you keep going a little longer?" He unfurled a roll of wires, all with different colored ends.

"Yeah. But… work fast." I was starting to feel the exertion now.

He didn't reply, just set to work.

Another firefighter and a cop skidded down the hill, carrying more gear.

"What do you want us to do, Mark?" the firefighter, Willy Baumgartner, asked.

"Start bagging. And radio up top to send a hose down."

The smoke had increased, and Delaney could see a faint orange glow from within the depths of the wreckage.

"Is anyone else in the car?" Jed Kauffman, the cop, asked.

"No," I said on an exhale. "Not… that I saw."

He walked out of my field of vision and toward the car.

The acetate sheet holding the cardiac lead stickers wobbled as Mark attached the wires to them. He shuffled closer on his knees. "Stop for a second, Delaney."

Gladly. I let the man's chest recoil from my last pump and sat back, breathing hard. Holy cow. I should just buy some squishy foam and do that for a workout. Forget the treadmill.

I swiped at the sweat on my face with the back of my forearm, watching Mark and his colleague work. With a set of trauma shears, Mark sliced through the man's dress shirt. The light blue cotton fell away. I expected him to start attaching the leads, but he paused, staring down at the guy's bare chest.

Suddenly, he glanced toward the police officer looking in the car. "Jed."

The man turned.

"This guy's been stabbed."

The sweat on my face turned to ice. He'd been *what*?

Four

G aze unfocused, I took a sip of the water a police officer brought me earlier and stared off into the distance while I waited for the detective to come talk to me. He'd shown up forty-five minutes ago, looked at me when one of the other officers pointed my direction, then walked down the hill and out of sight.

A yawn threatened, but I stifled it. If I started that, I'd never stop. I just wanted to go home, take a hot, hot shower, and crash. After the adrenaline rush of everything that occurred, then the trek back to the road, I was *done*.

But at least waiting around had given me time to arrange for my truck to get towed to town. Jed, the officer who'd been first on scene with the firefighters, had arranged it when he called for a company to come haul the dead man's car out of the ravine.

Dead.

The guy I'd worked so hard to save was dead.

Mark had tried to revive him after I stopped, shocking him several times, but to no avail.

I couldn't help but wonder what happened to him. Who was he and who had stabbed him? And why?

The stab wounds certainly explained why he'd careened over the hillside, though. If he wasn't already unconscious when he went over, he was probably close. There were no skid marks on the road. He hadn't even tried to slow.

His poor family.

I'd seen the wedding ring on his finger. I couldn't help but wonder about them and what would happen. How would they take the news?

Heaving a sigh, I took another sip of water. So many "what ifs." None of them mattered to me, personally, but I still couldn't help but worry about them.

"Ms. Fowler?"

I startled, making the water in my bottle slosh as I jumped. Straightening, I glanced up to see the detective from earlier approaching.

I gave him a quick once over.

He was quite the handsome man. A sharp angular jawline, patrician's nose, and deep dark eyes sat under a head of thick black hair. His complexion held olive undertones, suggesting some Mediterranean heritage. So did the hint of dark shadow on his cheeks and jaw.

As he walked closer, my head tipped back. He wasn't short, either.

"I'm Detective Jack Fiore. You witnessed the accident?"

I nodded, standing so I didn't feel quite so intimidated. He hadn't sat next to me, and I didn't like feeling so small.

"Can you walk me through what happened?"

"Um…" I rolled my lips in, thinking. "My truck broke down." I turned my head, nodding toward my food truck still sitting in the midst of the emergency vehicles. The tow truck driver promised me he would haul it down just as soon as all the other cars moved.

"I couldn't get a phone signal to call for help, so I started walking up the road to higher ground. I heard the car coming, so I crossed the street to be more visible to the car that came around the curve. Except he didn't slow and went over the side."

"He didn't slow at all?"

I shook my head. "No. I remember waiting to hear the engine noise change as he approached the bend and that didn't happen. He just whizzed past the corner and went straight over."

"Okay. What happened then?"

"I ran over to see how far down the car went. When I realized it was practically at the bottom, I called for help before climbing down."

"You had a signal then?"

"A bar, yes. I think the mountain was blocking it before." I pointed over my shoulder to the rock face behind me. "After I called 9-1-1, I went down the hill to see how I could help."

"The firefighters said you were doing CPR when they arrived. You know how foolish it was for you to climb down there, right? Without safety equipment? And then there was the danger that the car could catch fire and explode."

The admonition in his dark gaze made me bristle. Narrowing my eyes, I stared him down. "I know, but it wasn't *that* dangerous to climb down. There are plenty of trees to hang on to." I decided not to mention how I hadn't done that at first. "And I couldn't stop thinking, what if someone's in there, bleeding heavily? What if there are children in the car? I couldn't just stand up here and wait for help."

Some of the ire in his eyes softened. He nodded. "All right. Tell me what happened when you reached the car. Was the man conscious?"

"No. I called out several times on my way down as well as when I reached the car, but no one ever answered. Once I got to the vehicle and looked inside, he was slumped forward and there was blood all over his face. I checked for a pulse and didn't feel one, so I knew I needed to get him out."

"How did you do that, anyway? He's not a small man."

Color stained my cheeks. I shrugged. "Adrenaline? I'm not too sure, honestly. I just knew he needed help. I got the door to move enough yanking on it that I could wedge my foot in and use my legs to open it wider. Then I just kind of bear-hugged him and pulled."

"And that's how the firefighters found you? Doing CPR?"

"Yes."

"At any point, did you notice anyone else? Another car, perhaps, before you went down the hillside? Or a person running away from the crash?"

"N—" I started to say no, then frowned, remembering the figure at the top of the hill. "Actually, there was someone. After I reached the bottom. I heard a car and looked up, hoping someone had stopped to help. I don't know what happened, though. The car stopped and someone got out, because I saw a figure above me, but then they just left."

His gaze sharpened. "You're sure?"

"A hundred percent. There was a person standing at the top of the hill looking down. Then they disappeared, I heard a car door close, then the engine revving as they drove away." I crossed my arms, studying him. "Do you not want to write any of this down?"

"I'll summarize our conversation in a bit. Unless you have a physical description of the person you saw? That I'll write down now."

"No. I can't even tell you if it was a man or a woman. It was quick, and with the hour, the shadows were too thick to see much." There had still been plenty of daylight, but up here where the mountain and trees blocked the evening sun, it had been much darker.

"All right. Was there anything else unusual you noticed?"

I shook my head. "No. Just that. Do you know who the victim is?"

"We do. He had a wallet on him. I can't release that information yet, though. Not until we contact his next of kin."

"Oh." My brow furrowed, then my head bobbed. "Of course. That makes sense." I hugged myself a little tighter. While it did make sense that they wouldn't release the man's name until his family knew about his death, I'd hoped to know who it was. Now, it would just run in circles in my brain all night. Who in our community had died in such a tragic way? And who would have a reason to kill him?

Detective Fiore reached into his pocket and produced a white rectangle. "Give me a call if you remember anything else. Before you leave, I also need you to write out a witness statement. Deputy Kauffman can help you with that."

I took the business card. "Okay."

He took several steps back. "Have a good night, Ms. Fowler, and thank you for your efforts today."

I offered him a tremulous smile as he turned away, then fought an eye roll. My night would be just peachy.

Heaving another long sigh, I shoved the card into my pocket and went back to my rock to wait for the tow truck.

I leaned forward, resting an elbow on my leg and propping my chin on my fist. I'd already spoken to the tow truck driver. They planned to bring two trucks to haul the Mercedes up the mountainside, but he said they could haul my food truck anywhere I wanted it to go after they accomplished that. Which meant I had to hang around at least until they got here so I could give him my keys.

Once they arrived, I would call one of my sisters for help. I still needed to offload the baked goods I didn't sell. Some of them needed to be refrigerated. Others, I just didn't want to leave in a non-climate-controlled area overnight. But I didn't want to do that if we'd just have to sit around, waiting for the driver. It wouldn't take that long to unload, and I knew they would be on-scene for a while. Removing the car in the ravine wouldn't be a simple job.

An hour and twelve minutes later, and after watching a crime scene van and a coroner's van arrive, two tow trucks turned up. One was the size of a bus and had a long boom arm. The other wasn't much shorter, but its boom wasn't as long. As the drivers got out to talk to the firefighters and police, I got up and wandered over.

The driver from the bigger truck walked toward the ruined guardrail and peered down, shining a flashlight toward the wreck. I walked close enough just in time to hear him let out a low whistle.

"That's gonna be a job," he said.

Letting him assess the situation, I moved off to the side and called Darcy, my younger sister. The line rang several times before it rolled to voicemail. I hung up without leaving a message. It was hard to tell where she was or what she was doing. Of the three of us, she was the free spirit.

My thumb hovered over Daphne's name in my contacts. I didn't want to interrupt her evening if she'd managed to pull Morgan away from work.

So, I scrolled and found my best friend's name.

Scarlett Roberts and I had been best friends since second grade when we bonded on the playground over hot pink scrunchies and unicorn stickers.

I put the phone to my ear and listened to it ring.

Please pick up.

If Scarlett didn't answer, I'd have to call my parents. I loved them, and they were great, but they weren't evening people. Mom was often in her pajamas by seven. She and Dad would watch some television together before heading to bed around nine or so. It was already eight-thirty.

"Hello?"

"Oh, thank God! Scarlett, I need your help."

"Delaney? What's wrong?"

"I broke down on Amherst Road, then there was a car accident because some guy got stabbed and now he's dead. It's going to be a few hours before the tow truck company can haul my truck into town. Can you come pick me up and help me unload what baked goods I have left?"

Several beats of silence passed over the air waves.

"I'm sorry. Did you say someone got stabbed?"

I sighed. "Yeah. It's a long story. Can you just come up here?"

"Of course. You said Amherst?"

"Yeah. Just past Roland heading into town. Bring your hand truck. We're going to have to walk the stuff past the police line to your car." I had one, but I left it at the church. I never had reason to take it with me, and it just took up space in the truck, anyway. Scarlett owned a small boutique downtown, so she had one she used to move inventory around.

"Okay. I'll be there as quick as I can."

This time, my shoulders sagged with relief. "Thank you."

"Not a problem. See you soon."

We said our farewells and hung up.

Relieved I had a plan and wouldn't be here until midnight, I let a deputy know I had someone coming to help me, then found my rock once more and settled in to wait.

The roadway turned into a hive of activity as I sat there. The tow truck drivers began drawing out cable. One of them —the younger one—donned a hard hat and started the long side-stepping journey down the mountainside. About ten minutes after he disappeared, a firefighter used the wire from the second, smaller tow truck to take a rescue basket down. It looked like they were going to bring the body up with the winch. Which, quite honestly, was smart. That was a long way to carry something so heavy up such a steep slope by hand.

"This is crazy!"

I glanced over at the sound of Scarlett's voice. She was coming toward me, glancing over her shoulder at the two tow trucks as she pushed her little hand cart.

Rising from my rock, I met her halfway. "Yeah. It's quite the production."

She looked at me, concern drawing her eyebrows together. "You're all right, though? You're not hurt?"

My butt throbbed where I fell on the rock and my upper body ached from the exertion of the climb and the CPR, but it was nothing some painkillers, a hot bath, and some rest wouldn't fix. "No, I'm fine. I just watched it all happen."

"That's a relief. So, what happened to your truck?"

I steered her toward said food truck. "I don't know. The fuel pump, maybe? It kept skipping, then it finally sputtered and died. I couldn't make it up the hill."

"And then you just happened to witness an accident?"

"Yeah. But it wasn't an accident. The guy had been stabbed. The cops don't know if he was already dead when the car went over. But he was certainly out of it enough to not know what was going on, if he was still alive. He never tried to stop."

"That's nuts."

"Yep." Just talking about it brought back the shock of seeing those stab wounds. I was still a little shaky.

"Well, let's get all your stuff loaded into my car and get out of here. Let the police do their job. Who's running the investigation?" She turned her head, craning her neck to see who all was hanging around the scene. "Is Isaiah here?"

"Not that I saw." Scarlett's cousin was a police officer. "But I've been pretty out of it from the shock of it all. I remember seeing Jed Kauffman—he was the first deputy on scene—and Detective Fiore."

"Oh." Scarlett's eyes grew round. "You met him? What's he like? Isaiah pointed him out to me the other day, but I didn't get to talk to him. He's… pretty."

"You think?" I mean, I'd noticed, but I wasn't about to sit here and salivate over the man.

Scarlett rolled her eyes. "Yes, I think. What's he like?"

I lifted a shoulder. "He was pleasant enough, I suppose. Business-like." I reached for the back door on my truck and used my keys to unlock it. "He was a bit upset with me because I didn't stay on the road after I called in the accident. Told me I could have gotten hurt going down there to help that man." I rolled my eyes as I opened the door. "Like I could stay put when there was the possibility I could help someone who needed it?"

She chuckled. "He'll learn if he's around you enough."

A smile tilted one side of my mouth. I glanced over my shoulder at her as I stepped into the vehicle. "I doubt he'll be around me enough."

"Hey. Never say never."

"Letty, the only way I'll ever be around that man a bunch is if he's investigating me for something. I am not his type."

"How do you know what his type is? You only talked to him for a few minutes." Scarlett stepped inside behind me.

I pulled open the first drawer, using tongs to move pastries from the trays to bakery boxes. "He's tall, dark, and handsome. Like model handsome. I'm just me."

Scarlett sighed and grabbed an empty box. "Stop selling yourself short."

"I'm not. I'm being realistic. Besides, I'm not in the market for a man. Can we talk about something else, please?"

"Such as?"

"My sister's getting married."

Scarlett's hand froze, a cinnamon twist caught between the tongs she held. "What? Daphne or Darcy?"

"Daphne. Who would Darcy be marrying?"

"I don't know." Scarlett lifted a shoulder and resumed her boxing efforts. "But I wouldn't put it past her to spring spontaneous nuptials on your family."

I huffed a soft laugh. "True." Darcy was… Darcy. She let the wind push her wherever it wanted to blow. I was truly amazed she still lived in town and not in some commune somewhere. Though, I guess her house and property were her own little commune. She'd turned her little woodland property into an off-gridder's dream.

"So, have they set a date?"

"Mid-October. She wants me to make her cake."

"That's quick."

"She wants a fall wedding and doesn't want to wait. I can't really blame her." I removed another tray. "I'd probably do the same thing in her shoes if it was feasible. I mean, why wait, right?"

"Right. Has she said anything about dresses yet?"

"No. But she might stop in to talk to you. With the timeline she's on, she might decide to go with something vintage, and no one can source gorgeous vintage clothing like you, so…"

Scarlett grinned. "Aww, you flatter me." She laid a hand on her chest and fluttered her eyelashes.

I laughed. "Never. It inflates your ego."

Scarlett's laughter joined mine.

For the next fifteen minutes, we worked to unload the cases and box everything up. I usually did this back at the church, but I didn't want to transport things in her car on trays. It would all slide around and off the metal sheets.

"You have a lot left."

"I made a little extra. I was supposed to have a breakfast rally tomorrow, so I doubled up on the muffins and bagels." A frown creased my forehead. I needed to call the community services lady and tell her I couldn't make it. Shoot. I should have done that while I waited around.

"You can still go. Just load up your car instead. I'm sure people will understand."

I wrinkled my nose. "Yeah, but it doesn't look very good to sell things off the back of my car. It's sketchy, you know?"

"Maybe, but most people know you now. I don't think it'll be a problem."

I bit my lip, considering that. "You think?"

Her head bobbed. "I do. It might even make people more sympathetic, and they might buy more. You should try it. It can't hurt."

I hummed. "I'll think about it." She made valid points, and I certainly didn't want to miss out on the income. Especially not now with a mechanic's bill looming over me.

"I'll even come help. You said breakfast, right? I don't have to open the shop until eleven."

"You're sure?"

"Of course I'm sure."

I wouldn't turn away assistance. Not when it would be a weird day, working from my car. "Okay. You're on."

Scarlett grinned. "I'll bring the coffee."

Five

Buzzing filled my ears the next morning. Blinking slowly, I rolled over and slapped at my alarm clock with a groan. I did not want to get up.

Even with Scarlett's help, it had been after ten by the time I finished up at the church and got home. I'd planned to be in bed by about eight-thirty last night. Four-thirty a.m. came early.

Sitting up, I shoved the light blue coverlet off.

Millie trilled and hopped down. In the light spilling in under the door from the hallway nightlight, I could see her tail shake and twitch as she stalked away.

"Sorry, Mills," I muttered.

With a wide yawn, I stood and padded over the blue and cream floral rug to the door. She scampered out ahead of me, probably headed for her food bowl. I detoured into the bathroom.

Flipping on the light, I winced at the brightness reflecting off the white tile walls, then winced again when I caught sight of myself in the mirror. "Geez, girl. You look like a corpse." Dark circles rimmed my eyes, making my already pale skin seem even paler. It was not a pretty look. Concealer would be my friend today.

I reached into the shower and turned the water on, letting it warm while I brushed my teeth. Stripping out of my pajamas, I stepped into the spray and sighed as the heat enveloped me.

For several long minutes, I stood under the water, using my poof to soap my body. I'd been so tired last night I'd just fallen into bed. This was a nice way to wake up.

After rinsing off and shaving my legs, I shampooed and conditioned my hair. By the time I was done, I was much more awake and had some color to my skin, though the dark circles still decorated my face.

Quickly, I smeared on some concealer and dusted my cheeks with some blush. I'd put on lip balm later. After I ate.

Millie gave me a squinty-eyed glare and meowed at me from her perch on a maple barstool as I flipped on the kitchen light.

"Sorry. I know it's early." I glanced down at her food dish, noticing it was empty. Was it like that last night?

It might have been. That would account for some of her attitude this morning.

Walking into the pantry, I found the plastic container I kept her food in and brought it out to fill her dish. She jumped down off the stool, rubbing her head against my hand and meowing again.

I scratched her ears after dumping a couple of scoops into the gray ceramic bowl. "There you go, sweet girl." Rising, I took her water dish with me to fill it.

With the cat taken care of, I set about making my own breakfast—a frozen egg, cheese, and bacon burrito. And coffee. Scarlett promised to bring me some, but the rally didn't start for a couple of hours. I couldn't wait that long.

Putting a pod into the coffee machine, I hit start, then tossed the burrito onto a plate and into the microwave. After nuking it to the molten stage, I wrapped it in a fresh piece of foil and threw it into my tote. By the time I got to the church, it would be the perfect temperature. I could eat it while I gathered supplies.

"All right. You be good, Mills. I'll see you this afternoon." I planned to come home between my breakfast gig and my dinner gig. Laundry called my name.

Millie didn't look up from where she had her face buried in her bowl.

I chuckled as I picked up my tote. "I see where I stand. It's fine." Smiling, I left the house.

As the silence in the car surrounded me, my mind wandered to last night. I still had questions. Lots of them. Most importantly, who was the man in the car?

Winding my way through the dark, I continued to ponder what I'd seen, hoping a clue would surface. But I'd been over every second of last night. I still didn't remember anything new.

I slowed at the intersection by the church, then turned the corner and pulled into the parking lot. My headlights swept over another vehicle, and I frowned. That was Daphne's car. What was she doing here?

I parked next to her and got out. She met me at the front of our cars.

"What are you doing here?" I frowned, staring at her in the glow from the pole light on the corner of the lot.

"Tell me what you saw last night."

"What?" My frown intensified at both the wobble in Daphne's voice and at her question. "Why?" My eyes widened as it dawned on me why she might be asking. "Do you know who was in the car?"

"Yes." The word came out on a broken whisper.

"Who?"

"Morgan's boss. Phil Brunswick."

Recognition clicked in my brain. I knew he'd looked

vaguely familiar, but between the blood, the adrenaline, and the deathly pallor to his skin, I hadn't been able to place him.

"Delaney, the police showed up last night. Really late. They hauled Morgan down to the police station."

"What?" I breathed. "Come on." I stepped forward, ushering her toward the door. "Let's talk while I bake. You can help. It'll soothe your nerves."

Daphne blew out a breath. "Yeah, maybe."

There was no maybe about it. My sisters might not bake professionally, but they still baked. More than once, we'd had a baking party when one of us needed to destress a bit. I'd give her a bowl of dough she could punch down or a batch of muffins to mix up and watch the stress melt away.

Unlocking the door, I let us inside. As we descended the steps, I flipped the lights on.

"So, what happened?" I asked. "Why did the police take him in?" I prayed he had nothing to do with his boss's murder.

"I'm not too sure, actually. He got home about half an hour ago. The police showed up around eleven-thirty and asked him to come down to the station for questioning about Phil's death. I guess they found Morgan's wallet in Phil's car."

My hand froze in the act of setting my tote down. "His wallet?"

She nodded. "He told me yesterday evening he lost it. He thought maybe he dropped it at the food truck rally. I was going to swing by the front desk at the outpatient center today and see if anyone turned it in. Anyway, he thinks now it fell out of his pocket when he went with Phil to a client meeting. The cops, they"—she broke off to swallow hard—"they think he had something to do with Phil's death. They… argued yesterday. Pretty intensely."

"About what?" My bag hit the counter with a thud.

"That case. The one he took the phone call for?"

I nodded, remembering. Moving to the fridge, I grabbed several boxes of butter. We'd start with scones. They were quick to mix up and Daphne could slice and dice the butter with the pastry cutter. It would give her something to work out her frustrations on.

"Phil wanted him to take a dinner meeting yesterday. This was after he dumped a morning meeting on him that cut our evening short when we got engaged. Normally, Morgan doesn't mind the last-minute calls, but he'd had the proposal planned for weeks, then Phil dumped that client in his lap. They wanted a meeting yesterday morning, and he had to prep for it, so he went to the office after our date, and I went home." Daphne ran a hand through her dark blonde hair. "When this dinner meeting came up, wrecking our plans again, Morgan told me he threatened to quit."

"Oooo. I'm guessing his boss didn't like that?" I opened my flour canister and measured some into a bowl.

"No. Not at all. It would mean he'd have to cancel his own plans." She rolled her eyes. "Anyway, Phil demanded Morgan come in regardless, then threatened to fire him instead. Morgan told him to go ahead, then left."

"So, did he actually quit?"

Daphne threw her hands up. "I don't know. He never formally said he was, but he did walk out."

"I take it there were other people present to tell the police about this argument?" Closing the flour canister, I opened the sugar.

"Yeah. Phil's wife was there."

I arched my eyebrows. "In the middle of the day?" I knew Phil Brunswick's wife, Felicity, through various charity events we'd both been a part of. She typically steered clear of anything that even smelled of work.

"I know, right? We usually only ever see her at parties. But Morgan said she stopped in to bring Phil a file he forgot."

My eyebrows went even higher. If I'd ever harbored any

thoughts of hiring Phil as my lawyer, that bit of information would have smothered them. "He let his snoop of a wife—who has no legal background and doesn't work for him—bring him a case file?" I closed the sugar canister, then quickly added the last of the dry ingredients to the scone mix.

"Yep." Daphne accepted the bowl and sticks of butter I passed her.

"I wonder whose dirty laundry Felicity will air around town next?"

"Right?" She opened the butter and dumped it in the bowl. "It's ridiculous."

"Is Morgan home now?"

"Sort of." Daphne picked up the pastry cutter and jabbed it into the scone mix. "Since I was there when the police arrived, I stayed at his house, waiting for him to get home. He gave me a brief rundown, then left for the office. He and the other attorneys were going to contact all their clients and postpone anything that wasn't strictly necessary."

"At this hour, they were going to do that?"

"I think they need to go through all of Phil's cases, too, so they can determine who's taking over what. And the cops need information on his clients. Everyone's a suspect right now." She stabbed the dough and twisted the pastry cutter. "I told him I hope they're looking extra hard at Felicity and not getting wrapped up with him. If anyone murdered him, it's her."

I frowned, in the middle of mixing up a second batch of scones. "Why?"

"Because I heard he threatened to cut her off. I guess her spending was getting out of control."

I could believe that. Felicity Brunswick liked the finer things in life.

"Who'd you hear that from?"

"Some of the older ladies who are part of the country club. A couple of them come in for physical therapy at the same time. They gossip while they do their exercises. I've learned a lot about the movers and shakers of this town since they started coming in."

I let out a soft snort. "I bet."

She chuckled. "They're a fount of information. I just stand there, pretending not to listen, and learn so much. Probably more than I want to know."

"They'll come in handy, now, though. I'm sure they'll have the inside scoop on the entire investigation."

"Maybe." Daphne's brows knit together. "Morgan said the new detective is… different."

"Detective Fiore?"

She nodded.

"How so?"

Daphne lifted a shoulder. "He just said he seemed more intense than the other officers he's dealt with. I'm wondering if that will mean he keeps things a little closer to the vest."

It was my turn to frown. "Maybe." I thought about my first impression of the detective. He'd definitely seemed intense. Maybe it would mean he'd keep his cards close. I didn't know anything about him.

An idea took root in my brain and began percolating.

I wonder if he likes scones…

Morgan did. I could take some to both of them. See what each of them knew about Phil Brunswick's last hours. And hey, who didn't like fresh baked goods? Maybe it would brighten both their days.

"How's this?"

Daphne's question snapped me out of my thoughts. I stepped over and looked in her bowl. "Looks good. Trade me." I picked up the new mix and handed it to her, along with some butter, then took what she'd stirred together.

"I just don't know what to think or do about all this. I know Morgan didn't do it, but the police can't rule him out based on a *feeling*," Daphne said, dumping butter into the bowl.

"Were you with him around the time of Phil's death?" I moved to the fridge to get the milk.

"No. I was getting ready for our date. I had late patients yesterday, so I didn't get off work until almost seven. We met for dinner at seven-thirty."

I wrinkled my nose as I shut the refrigerator door. That meant Morgan didn't have an alibi.

"What did you see?" Daphne asked. "Was there anything that could offer a clue about who did this?"

"The only thing I saw, other than his car go flying over the edge, was someone standing at the top of the hill, then leaving." Quickly mixing up the wet ingredients, I added them and some sliced almonds to the batter.

"You saw someone?"

"Yes. But I can't tell you who or even if it was a man or a woman. It was just a fleeting glimpse." I set the mixing bowl on the mixer stand and turned it on, giving it a quick whisk to combine everything. Shutting off the machine, I removed the bowl. "I told Detective Fiore all of this."

"What did he say?"

"Not much. Thank you, basically."

Daphne sighed. "And you didn't notice anything else?"

I shook my head as I dumped the dough out onto the floured counter. "No. I didn't even recognize Phil. He was covered in blood and just—he didn't look like himself." I tried not to picture it. It had kept me awake enough last night. I'd finally banished the image and didn't want it to come back.

Her mouth flattened. "Darn. I was hoping you knew something."

"I'm sorry." I sent her an apologetic look as I separated the scone dough into four equal piles using my food scale.

She waved a hand. "Don't be. I knew coming here, it

would be a long shot. But I just had to know what you knew. It wasn't like I was sleeping, anyway."

Sympathy tugged at my heart. "Did you get any rest?" I pulled a sheet of parchment over one pile of dough, then picked up my rolling pin.

"Not really. I think I dozed for a bit on the couch around three. Morgan got home just before four. He startled me awake when he came in, that I remember. I tried to get him to stay. To get some sleep, but he told me he was too keyed up, and that he and the others needed to go through files and contact clients. He was only home for about fifteen minutes. Long enough to give me a quick rundown of what happened while he changed clothes. I came here right after he left."

With the dough now flattened, I peeled the parchment off and patted it into a roughly circular shape, then picked up my knife to cut it into eight equal wedges.

"I'm just worried about him. I could tell he was upset." She sifted her fingers through the crumbly mixture in her bowl, then pushed it toward me. "This was supposed to be the happiest time of my life." Her face crumpled and tears formed in the corners of her eyes. "But I can't enjoy it because —because—" She stopped and waved a hand, too choked up to continue.

I set my knife down and walked over to her, folding her into a hug. "I'm sorry, Daph." I wished I could offer her more. That I'd seen more, so she could stop worrying that her fiancé would get framed for something he didn't do. But I couldn't.

She hugged me back, then eased away. "I'm sorry too. I'm being melodramatic."

"You're fine. You're allowed to be upset."

She wiped at her face. "I know. It's all just ridiculous."

I couldn't help but agree. Morgan was not a murderer.

"Can we talk about something else? I don't want to dwell on this anymore right now."

"Of course." I moved away, an idea striking me. "How

about we design your wedding cake?" I walked over to my tote and withdrew a sketchbook. It was something I carried everywhere. Sometimes, inspiration struck out of nowhere, and I wanted to be prepared. It also helped pass the time at rallies when business was slow.

Daphne sniffed and wiped the last of the moisture from her face. "Sure."

I flipped to a blank page and dug a pencil from my bag. "All right. Let's start with tiers. How many do you want?"

"Four, I think. We'll probably need that much cake, right?"

"Maybe. I'm sure people will take it home, though, if it's not all eaten at the reception. Okay, what shape? Round?"

"Yes."

I sketched out a quick four-tier round cake. "Primary color?"

Daphne groaned. "I don't know."

I glanced up. "Do you know what colors you want to use for your bridesmaids' dresses and for flowers?"

"Sort of." Her mouth twisted. "I was thinking a deep purple for the dresses. Or a dark crimson. Both of those are fall-ish. Then maybe adding some greens and golds. And cream, just so it's not so heavy."

An entire palette unfolded in my mind's eye. "What if you went with the dark crimson dresses? We could do the same color for the main frosting on the cake, then I could accent with an aqua color as well as gold and cream. And for your flowers and other decorations, you could use the cream as your main color, then accent with crimson and aqua. And gold, too, of course. I think that would look really nice. I know you like purple, but if you want greens in there, I think the purple will look too summery." I reached for the drawer where I kept my food coloring and removed several tubes in the colors I was thinking.

"Here. These." I laid them out for her. "And if you don't

like that green, we could go with something more like this." I pulled a more minty color from the drawer.

"Those would be flowers?" She pointed at the greens.

"Possibly. Or I could use it as just accent piping. It's up to you and how realistic you want the cake to look. I could also do a leafy design and use colors more like... these." I pulled several plant-colored greens from my drawer.

She groaned again. "Stop giving me so many options."

I chuckled. "That's my job."

She rolled her eyes.

"Why don't you take a picture of these colors and when you have some spare time, go online and find a few cakes you like. Search the colors, but also search for, like, cakes with leaves and cakes with gold accents. Mix it up. You'll be surprised at what you'll find."

Daphne inhaled a deep breath, holding it for a moment before she blew it out. "Yeah. Okay. I'll do that sometime today. Maybe on my lunch break. It'll help distract me."

I laid a hand on her shoulder. "No rush. Well, there's a bit of a rush." I held my fingers up, about an inch apart, then smiled.

My levity had the desired effect, and she smiled back.

"Okay. How about by the end of the weekend?"

I closed my sketchbook. "It's your wedding. You do it when you have the time. I just need a couple weeks' notice to make the cake. Three if you plan to make it super elaborate. I was thinking more about you nailing down a color scheme, so you can have flowers ordered and start looking at decorations. And dresses. I'm assuming I need a bridesmaid's dress for this?"

"Yeah," she breathed. "I guess there really is a lot to do, isn't there?"

"Yep."

Daphne pulled her lower lip between her teeth, nibbling on it. "Maybe we should wait until next year."

"Oh, no." I waved my hands. "Let's not start second-guessing things. It can be done. Will it be a crazy, chaotic mess? Yes. But it's doable. I'm guessing you're having it on the inn's grounds?" Our parents owned the Fernwood Inn, a bed-and-breakfast right on the lake.

She nodded. "That was the plan."

"So, you already have the most important thing checked off the list. The venue." I ticked it off my fingers. "Come up with colors, figure out who all your bridesmaids are, and we'll go dress shopping."

Daphne reached out, gathering me into a tight hug. "What would I do without you?"

I hugged her back. "Ask Mom for help."

Laughing, she pulled back. "I'll probably do that, anyway. She'll be better at keeping track of all the little details than any of us."

That was the truth. Our mom's lists had lists.

I gave her another quick squeeze. "Don't worry, okay? Everything—and I mean everything—will work out just fine."

"I sure hope so." Moisture gathered in her eyes again. "It's just all so overwhelming, you know? I mean, how am I supposed to think about putting a wedding together when my groom is suspected of murdering his boss?" She fanned her face. "Sorry. Ignore me. I said I didn't want to think about it, and I don't. It'll work out, you're right."

"You're darn right, I'm right." I offered her a bright smile as determination filled my chest. Not only would I create the most beautiful wedding cake Fernwood had ever seen, I would make sure the groom was there to see it.

No one—and certainly not some stern-faced detective—would pin a murder on Morgan.

I'd make sure of it.

$$Six$$

Armed with a bakery box filled with a half-dozen almond scones and another half-dozen freshly baked cinnamon rolls, I hip bumped my car door shut. Fumbling with my keys, I hit the lock button, then looked up at the façade of Morgan's office building. With my breakfast rally over—and quite successful despite the circumstances—I was off to do a little information gathering.

Brunswick & Flaherty Law was housed in a quaint three-story brick Victorian. Cream gingerbread trim decorated the wide front porch and the apex of the roof. A pair of rocking chairs and a small table sat to one side of the front door, along with some large potted ferns. It was homey and cute—the opposite of what I would expect from someone like Phil Brunswick.

Nile Flaherty, on the other hand, exuded a calmness and an "I'm a hometown guy" sort of appeal that fit right in with the décor. I'd met him a couple of times since Daphne began dating Morgan. How Flaherty and Brunswick became business partners I didn't know. I think Morgan mentioned they met in law school. Flaherty was a local. Brunswick, though, was originally from Seattle.

My shoes made soft scuffing sounds on the concrete walkway as I moved toward the building. The sound changed to soft, hollow thuds as I ascended the wooden porch steps and crossed to the door.

Turning the handle, I let myself inside.

I took a quick glance around the empty room. Like the porch, it was homey and comfortable. The front door opened into a small foyer. Directly ahead of me was a walnut staircase. Running along the right of the staircase was a long hallway that led to several rooms with closed doors.

An opening directly to my right led to what I assumed used to be the house's formal parlor. It was now a reception area. A fireplace with a marble mantle and cast-iron insert sat on the far wall. The deep jade tiles in the hearth set into the hardwood floor had a hint of a smoky color to them. Someone had pulled the color from them for the walls, which were painted a soft gray. Under the window, a set of gold damask wingback chairs flanked a small end table. No one sat at the large wooden desk on the rear wall of the room, but I could hear voices coming through the open door in the corner.

"Hello?" I stepped into the parlor, peering toward the door.

The voices ceased. A moment later, heels clacked on the floor and a woman appeared.

I felt my eyes widen at her appearance and quickly forced them back into compliance.

The woman looked like a supermodel.

Tall, even without the four-inch jet-black heels on her feet, miles of exposed leg were visible beneath the short black pencil skirt clinging to her butt and tiny waist. She'd gone a little more conservative on the top, with a black button-up that hugged her ample chest. Blonde tendrils falling out of the twist on the back of her head framed her face.

"Hello." She offered me a tight smile, stretching the pink

lipstick on her mouth. "I'm sorry, we're closed today. If you had an appointment, I'm happy to reschedule you."

"Oh, no. No appointment. I'm Morgan's fiancée's sister. I brought you all some goodies to help you through today." I held up the bakery box.

Her eyes narrowed, then a moment later, grew round. "Wait. Are you the one who—who—saw—" She stopped, swallowing hard. Moisture welled in her eyes.

"I am. I'm sorry. I didn't mean to make you upset."

The woman lifted a hand to her face, touching the end of her nose with the side of her pinkie. "It's all right. It still doesn't seem real yet, but every once in a while, it hits just right, you know?"

I hummed, sympathizing with her. "It's terrible, what happened."

Her head bobbed. "It is. Phil can—could—be a bit of a jerk sometimes, but he wasn't a bad man. I don't know why someone would want to do something so heinous." She blinked rapidly and pressed trembling fingers to her lips.

"So, you don't have any idea who would want to kill him?"

"No."

"What about a client? Or someone associated with a client? I'm sure some of the people and businesses he represented have enemies." The wheels in my mind turned. That made the most sense. It was the nature of a lawyer's job to make enemies. At least for those who did more than simple contracts, anyway. It was inevitable that eventually, someone on the opposing side would get upset. Maybe even upset enough to kill.

"I'm sure he's encountered people who don't appreciate what he does. This new client—"

"Mandi, could you help Tara with sorting correspondence, please?" An older gentleman I would guess to be about Phil Brunswick's age stepped through the doorway.

The woman turned at the sound of the man's voice. "Oh. Yes, of course." She took a step toward him, then hesitated, glancing at me.

"I'll take care of her. You go help Tara."

"All right." Mandi lifted a hand. "It was nice to meet you, miss."

"You too." I offered her a polite smile.

The man stepped to the side to allow her to pass. Once she was gone, he turned to me. "I'm Nile Flaherty, a senior managing partner here. I'm sure Mandi told you we're closed today. If you need an appointment, please call us next week. We'll be happy to help you."

"Oh, I'm not here to make an appointment. I just came to check on Morgan and to offer you all my condolences. Morgan is my sister's fiancé. I brought these for all of you as well." Again, I lifted the bakery box.

The politely blank expression on his face turned curious. There was something else in his eyes, too, that I couldn't name. It was a hard note, but I didn't know what it meant.

"Are you the sister who saw Phil's accident and tried to help?"

"I am."

He walked closer.

My spine straightened as he stopped within a couple of feet. I curled my hands over the edge of the box, tucking it into my stomach to use as a barrier between us. With that hard stare on his face, he was entirely too close for my comfort.

"What did you see?"

"Nothing, really. I—" I stopped abruptly as he took another step in my direction. His abdomen nearly touched my fingers now. I planted my feet, refusing to let him intimidate me.

"Who else was there? Someone did this. You had to have seen who it was." He leaned in.

"No. Really, I didn't." I glared up at him. Is this how he won cases? Intimidated witnesses and bullied people? Daphne said he was the nice one of the two senior partners. I didn't believe it. They both seemed like jerks. "Would you mind backing up? I don't like people in my personal space."

He held my gaze for several beats. I stared right back. Who did he think he was?

The door behind me opened.

Immediately, Mr. Flaherty straightened, the carefully blank and polite expression returning to his face as he faced the newcomer.

I turned and blinked in surprise. It was Detective Fiore.

He spotted me and frowned. "Ms. Fowler? What are you doing here?"

For the third time, I indicated the bakery box. "Bringing a treat for the office. I'm sure by now you know Morgan Dean is my sister's fiancé."

"I do. How do you know I know Mr. Dean?"

I rolled my eyes. "Are you not from a small town, Detective? News travels fast. My sister was waiting for me when I got to work this morning. Actually, she helped me make the scones in here." I tapped the box with a finger. A box I was tired of holding.

Turning, I looked at Mr. Flaherty. "If you don't mind, I'm going to go give this to Morgan." I moved to step around him.

"Actually, I do mind. We have sensitive information back there. You can set it on Mandi's desk." He pointed to the piece of furniture.

I narrowed my eyes at him. If he wanted to play the petty game, so could I. "Oh, you mean sensitive information like what Mrs. Brunswick brought to her husband from home yesterday? That kind of sensitive information?" I held his gaze until I stepped around him. He just glared at me.

What a dirtbag.

Shifting my grip on the box, I moved to set it down. Mandi's desk calendar caught my eye. In the square for yesterday, she'd written "PB mtg w/Hickman 8am."

PB? Phil Brunswick? Was he the only one here who had those initials? I didn't know, but I made a mental note to ask Morgan. And who was the Hickman in question? Hickman Energy Group? Was that Phil's client?

My mind whirled with the possibilities as I set the box down and straightened. Turning, I pasted a saccharine smile on my face as I looked at Mr. Flaherty. "Enjoy the scones and cinnamon rolls. I'm sorry for your loss."

Shoulders straight and head held high, I headed for the door.

"Ms. Fowler." Detective Fiore's low voice stopped me.

I glanced over my shoulder, giving him a questioning look.

"What did you mean by that comment?"

I frowned. "Which one?"

"The one about Mrs. Brunswick."

"And the sensitive information?"

He nodded.

"That's why she was here yesterday to witness Morgan and Mr. Brunswick argue. Daphne told me that Morgan said she'd stopped in to bring him some files he left at home."

Dark eyebrows rose on his handsome face. "Really. Well, that's interesting. She told me she just stopped in to say hello." He cast a side glance at Mr. Flaherty, who suddenly looked uncomfortable.

Satisfaction stirred in my gut, and I resisted the urge to jab a finger toward the detective and say, "See? Morgan isn't the only one you should be looking at." But I didn't. I behaved.

Instead, I just shrugged. "That's what I was told. I'll leave it to you to uncover the truth." I reached for the doorknob. "Have a good day." Pulling the door open, I exited without a backward glance.

A smile broke out on my way to the car. Oh, that felt glorious to stick it to Mr. Flaherty after the attitude he took with me! I hoped Detective Fiore grilled him mercilessly about the office policy on "sensitive material."

My car beeped as I unlocked it. I hopped in and fired up the engine. Buckling up, my gaze landed on the second bakery box sitting on the rear passenger seat. The one intended for Detective Fiore and the other sheriff's department staff.

I bit my lip as a new idea for the goodies formed.

Should I?

I mean, I really should go see Mrs. Brunswick and offer my condolences. I had intended to at some point soon. But now that I knew she lied? Was it wise to go?

Probably not.

I reached back for the box and set it on the passenger seat. Just because it wasn't wise didn't mean I wouldn't. Now more than ever, I wanted to see how she was coping with her husband's death. Morgan didn't kill him, but someone did. Maybe the reason she was at the office wasn't the only thing she lied about.

Pulling onto the main road, I headed away from the city center and back up into the hills. The Brunswicks lived in an exclusive neighborhood high on the mountainside in a gated community. I was hoping Mrs. Brunswick would let me inside.

Which was why I had treats. Food loosened people up.

It took me about fifteen minutes to reach the Brunswicks' neighborhood. I turned onto the road leading in and stopped at the gate. A simple search online had surprisingly yielded their address. I'd figured an attorney would keep that information private. Apparently, the location made Mr. Brunswick feel safe.

Rolling down my window, I pushed the button for their

house number under the small security camera lens and listened to the attached speaker ring several times.

A moment later, a woman's voice sounded, but it wasn't Felicity Brunswick. "Yes?"

"Hi, my name is Delaney Fowler. I'm here to see Mrs. Brunswick."

"She's not taking visitors."

"I'm the woman who tried to save her husband. And I brought treats." I reached for the bakery box and showed it to the fisheye lens.

"You—you're the woman who found Phil?" The woman's voice turned shaky.

"Yes."

"Please come in." The intercom clicked as she disconnected.

A moment later, the eighteen-foot wrought-iron gates swung inward.

I drove through.

It only took a couple of minutes to find the Brunswicks' house. I turned left off the road and wound through the trees, heading up for several hundred feet, before a sprawling stone and log home appeared.

"Dang. Did they ever even see each other in this monstrosity?" I parked under the portico over the drive, grabbed the bakery box, and got out.

The house looked more like a lodge-style resort than a single-family home. River stone columns held up the giant cedar beams supporting the slate roof over the portico. The house stretched at least a hundred feet in either direction, the gray-brown siding fading into the landscape.

I approached the walnut double doors inset into two-story windows on either side. Through them, I could see inside and out the back of the house, which was nothing but a wall of glass. Locating the bell, I pushed it. A moment later, I saw a woman approaching.

One of the doors swung inward, revealing a woman in her late forties or early fifties whose appearance screamed wealth. Dressed in pressed khaki slacks and an ivory linen blouse, pearls shone below her collar and leather flats peeked out from the bottom of her pants. Her chestnut-colored hair was combed and styled to within an inch of its life. The perfect makeup on her face couldn't hide the redness in her eyes, though.

"Hi." I offered her a soft, sympathetic smile. "I'm Delaney Fowler."

"Skyler Brunswick-Taft. I'm Phil's sister." She stepped back. "Come in, please."

Entering the house, my eyes immediately went up, widening as I caught sight of the gigantic iron and glass chandelier hanging from the exposed rafters. It was dark now, thanks to the sun streaming in through the floor-to-ceiling windows, but I imagined in the evenings it lit up the entire great room.

"Let's sit, shall we?" Skyler held out an arm, motioning me toward the seating area in the middle of the room.

"Sure." I moved toward a large brown leather sofa and perched on one of the cushions, setting the box on the live-edge coffee table.

Skyler took a seat beside me, leaving almost a full cushion between us. "I want to say thank you for what you did. I know…" She trailed off, swallowing hard before continuing. "I know you weren't successful, but it still means a lot that you tried."

"I appreciate that. I couldn't just stand around and wait for help. How's his wife doing?"

"About as expected, I suppose. I came over when she called last night. After we spoke to the police, she went to bed and asked not to be disturbed. I haven't seen her yet today." She gave a soft smile. "Maybe your pastries will entice her out of her room."

I returned her smile and reached for the box. "Maybe." Setting it on my lap, I opened the lid. "It's some almond scones and some cinnamon rolls. I find both comforting, so that's what I made."

"They look delicious, thank you."

I closed the lid and put the box back on the table. "You're welcome. I'm so sorry for your loss."

Skyler sniffed, drawing a tissue from the pocket of her tan slacks. "Thank you. Phil will be missed." She dabbed at her eyes. "He could be a right bastard at times, but he was my brother and I loved him."

"I know how that goes. I have two sisters." Neither of whom I would ever class in the same manner as Skyler did Phil, but she didn't need to know that. I was here to find out more about Phil, and I wanted her to feel comfortable. "Do you know of anyone who would want to hurt him?"

She dabbed at her eyes again. "No. Well," she paused and glanced up, inhaling a breath. "I guess no one specific comes to mind. He made enemies just doing what he did for a living. And as I said, he could be, well, rude, quite frankly. Phil has"—she stopped, taking a shaky breath—"had a strong personality. He had rigid ideas about how things should be, how they should happen, and it was difficult to change his mind. Usually, he just powered through and did things the way he wanted. It didn't really win him any favors, you know?"

I nodded.

"He didn't have friends, really. More acquaintances. People who tolerated him because of who he was."

My brow wrinkled. "Was he aware of that fact?"

She sniffed and wiped at her nose. "Yes. But it didn't really bother him. He had what he wanted." She gestured to the house. "He valued possessions, like this house and his cars, more than most people."

I could not imagine living like that. My family was everything to me. I'd live in a dirt hut if it meant saving one of my sisters or my parents. "How does Mrs. Brunswick feel about that?"

Skyler scoffed and rolled her eyes. "Felicity is much the same. It's what made them such a good match." A sudden anger burned in her eyes. "She's probably more upset that her meal train has been cut off than she is over Phil's death."

I blinked, shocked. "Really?"

"Yes. His son from his first marriage will get most of his money. Oh, she'll get a generous inheritance from his estate, but with her tastes and lifestyle, she'll burn through the money in a few years. Then, she'll either need to sell the house or find some poor, rich sap to support her."

I cleared my throat. Well, then. "You don't seem to like your sister-in-law very much."

Skyler lifted a shoulder. "She's tolerable most days, but we're not best friends. I'm only here for her now because she doesn't really have anyone else to lean on."

"Well, that's very kind of you."

"Honestly? I'm just saving James—Phil's son—from having to put up with her. He's one of the few people Phil truly loved and cared about. He wouldn't want him to be burdened with Felicity's drama while he's grieving."

I ran my tongue over my teeth and nodded slowly. "Right."

"Anyway, that was the long answer to your question. No, I don't have any clue who would want to murder my brother. Like I said, he wasn't well-liked, but I don't think he was hated. Not enough for someone to kill, you know?"

I pressed my lips together. "Yeah. I guess it will be up to the police to really tear his life apart now. Since no one really sticks out."

"It will. I just hope the practice survives the fallout."

My expression quickly morphed to one of confusion.

"What do you mean?" Alarm bells clanged in my brain. Was something going on there that could put Morgan in danger?

Her expression closed. "Nothing. I just meant there will be a lot of scrutiny on Phil's partner and their employees. It could disrupt business."

I studied her for a moment. "I see. Well, I hope not. My sister's fiancé works there."

"Oh? That's certainly a coincidence."

I shrugged. "I guess so."

"Skyler?" A woman's voice carried through the room. "I heard the doorbell. Who stopped—"

I turned in my seat, meeting Felicity Brunswick's gaze.

"Oh." She glanced at her sister-in-law, her blue eyes flinty. "I thought I said I didn't want any visitors?"

Skyler glared back. "This is Delaney Fowler, the woman who tried to save Phil. I wanted to thank her for trying."

Felicity's jaw worked, and she lifted her nose slightly. "Well. Okay." She nodded to me, once. "Thank you."

I arched an eyebrow at the stiff words. "You're welcome."

"Come have a seat, Felicity." Skyler patted the couch next to her.

The younger woman hesitated, then, back straight, she walked closer, rounding the couch to sit in a wingback chair.

I smiled and nudged the bakery box toward her. "I brought you some pastries. Comfort food."

"I don't eat refined sugar or flour, but thank you."

I fought the urge to roll my eyes. Life was not worth living without baked goods. My butt didn't thank me for that philosophy, but my mental stability sure did. I looked at Skyler. "Well, then, I guess that's more for you."

"I'll take them home with me. My boys will devour them."

Felicity's lip curled in a slight sneer before she quickly schooled it back into its previously annoyed expression.

What was that all about?

"You can do that whenever you want, Skyler. I'm quite all right now."

"Are you sure? There are still funeral arrangements to be made. We also—"

Felicity waved a hand, cutting her off. "James can take care of that. He is the executor of Phil's will, after all." The sneer returned.

Anger reappeared in Skyler's eyes. "Yes. You're right, he is." Her spine straightened, and she lightly smacked her hands on her thighs. "Well, then, I guess I'll head home." She stood.

"You should go, too, Ms. Fowler. I'd like to be alone."

"Oh." My brow's dipped into a quick frown. "Of course. Okay." Rising to my feet, I glanced at Skyler and held out a hand. "It was nice to meet you. Again, I'm sorry for your loss." And for her, I'm sure it was a loss. She seemed to genuinely care about her brother.

Tears welled in the woman's eyes again, but she forced a bright smile and blinked them away as she took my hand. "Thank you. And thank you for the pastries."

"You're welcome. I hope your family enjoys them." Releasing her hand, I gave both women a quick wave as I backed toward the door.

"I'll show you out." Skyler moved to follow me.

"That's all right. I know the way." Smiling, I took another step back, then turned and headed for the front door.

Outside, I glanced through the windows, where I could see the two women still standing near the couch as I rounded the hood of my car to get in. Neither one paid me any heed. Instead, they faced each other. I could only see their profiles, but it was obvious they were arguing. Probably about me.

It had been quite apparent that Felicity didn't want me there. I doubted it was because she was grieving over Phil's death. Not if what Skyler said was true.

I reached for the driver's door handle, eyes still on the

house, when suddenly, Felicity swung at Skyler, slapping her across the face.

"Whoa," I whispered.

In the next moment, Skyler shoved her, sending her toppling onto the sofa. She took a step forward, a fist raised. I let go of the door handle, ready to run in and intervene. I might not like Felicity, but that didn't mean I wanted to see her get pummeled.

But Skyler slowly lowered her fist. She jabbed a finger in the air at her sister-in-law as she said something I couldn't hear, then snatched the bakery box off the table and stormed away.

"Wow." Shaking my head, I opened my driver's door and slipped into the seat.

That was one dysfunctional family.

$$\mathit{Seven}$$

After my enlightening conversations this morning, I drove to the repair shop to check on my truck. I was hoping it wouldn't be a long or expensive fix. My budget and my business couldn't handle either.

Turning into the parking lot, I saw it sitting in the larger of the shop's three bays. I could see the mechanic, Yves Taskin, bent over the engine compartment, shining a light inside. I didn't know whether to be happy or sad there weren't parts lying on the table beside him. Either way, I had confidence in him. At fifty-eight, Yves had decades of experience repairing all sorts of vehicles. He'd been a fixture in the community as long as I could remember. My parents had always taken their cars to him, so naturally, I did the same.

With a sigh, I picked up the third box I'd grabbed before I left the church kitchen—a half dozen chocolate chip cookies—and got out, then headed for the customer entrance. The bell jingled overhead as I entered. Through the wall of glass overlooking the garage, I saw Yves straighten and look my way.

I waved.

He backed away from the truck and grabbed a rag, wiping

his hands as he walked toward the lobby. As he neared, he offered me a sunny smile that reached his silvery-blue eyes.

My heart thumped. Did that mean he had good news?

Opening the glass door set into the wall of windows, he stepped into the lobby, tucking back a flyaway wisp of his silver hair that escaped the small bun at the back of his head. "Good morning, Delaney. Come to check on your bakery truck?"

I nodded. "What's the verdict?" I held my breath, hoping it was minor.

"I'm not a hundred percent certain yet, but from the way it sounds, I'm thinking it's the fuel pump. It died on a hill, right? That's what you said in your voice message, isn't it?"

"Yes. It did."

His head bobbed. "Yeah. It's having trouble pumping the fuel up, and on that incline, gravity wasn't its friend. I'll know more later this morning after I run a few more checks."

"Okay. Do you have a timeline yet on how long it'll take?"

"If I can diagnose the problem and get the parts ordered to be delivered this afternoon, I might be able to get it back to you yet today. Otherwise, it'll be Monday."

Hope lit my chest. That would be amazing if he could get it back to me today. I had a wedding this weekend. Popping up the back hatch of my SUV wasn't an option for an event like that. I didn't know what I'd do if I had to cancel it. "Okay. I'll get out of your hair, then, so you can get back to work. I brought you these." I lifted the box, then took a couple steps to the side to set it on the checkout desk. "Chocolate chip cookies."

His blue eyes crinkled at the corners as he gave me a delighted smile. "My favorite. Thank you, Delaney."

I returned his smile. "You're welcome, Yves." I headed for the door. "Work fast."

He chuckled. "I'll do my best."

With a wave, I left, buoyed by the news. I prayed it really was just the fuel pump and he could have it fixed today.

But I couldn't be too optimistic. I needed to make a contingency plan. Canceling really wasn't an option.

Back in my car, I drummed my fingers on the steering wheel as I thought. Mom and Dad had the van they used for the inn. Maybe they'd let me borrow it to transport my product. I could pack a couple of tables in there to set stuff up on. I might not be able to take items that needed to stay cold, but I could still bring most things. And a nice table display would be much more favorable for a wedding if I couldn't take my food truck. Of course, it would still be up to the bride and groom, but knowing them, I had a feeling they would be okay with that.

Nodding to myself, I started my car, then pointed it in the direction of my parents' inn.

Thirteen minutes later, I turned down the pine tree-lined lane leading to the property.

I pushed the button to roll down my window and took a deep breath. The crisp, clean, pine-scented air of home never failed to make me smile and lighten my worries.

Gravel crunched beneath my tires as I drove through the forest. Water splashed as I hit a puddle, a couple droplets landing on my arm. It only made me smile more. I loved this place.

My sisters and I had grown up running through these woods, splashing in puddles and soaking our clothes from the droplets that clung to the ferns and pine boughs. We had skipped rocks from the rough sand beach at the bottom of the hill and paddled kayaks on the lake. I'd been sad to move away from Fernwood Inn, but I'd needed my own space and a place that was all my own. While I no longer lived on the property, I was still a frequent visitor.

Emerging from the trees, I entered the clearing around the inn. Sunlight glinted off the large windows and made the log siding gleam a rich, golden brown. As I drove around the side of the building, the rear decks came into view. At this hour, they were mostly empty. Only a few guests sat at the tables, sipping coffee and eating the undoubtedly delicious breakfast prepared by both my parents.

My stomach rumbled. I could go for some of Dad's poached eggs and smoked salmon. I would wager a bet Mom made blueberry cream scones too.

It all sounded so good.

Turning, I pulled my car up beside the garage. Another day, perhaps, I would stay for breakfast. When I hadn't already eaten and didn't have quite so much to do.

I hopped out of my car and entered the inn through the garage, typing my code into the keypad to get inside. I did the same at the inner door and walked into the family kitchen.

My mom, standing at the sink rinsing breakfast dishes, looked over and smiled.

"Well, good morning. What are you doing here? Why aren't you working?"

I paused in the doorway and frowned. Slowly, I shut the door. "You didn't hear?"

"Hear what?" She rinsed the plate she'd just finished washing and set it in the dish rack to dry.

"Oh boy." I blew out a breath, ruffling my bangs. Taking three steps forward, I pulled out a stool at the island and sat down. "Buckle up. This is a doozy."

It took me ten minutes, but I went through what happened last night and my conversation with Daphne early this morning. I also touched on going to talk to Morgan and seeing Detective Fiore again. I left out visiting Felicity Brunswick, not wanting to get scolded for sticking my nose where it didn't belong.

Mom dried her hands on a towel, then leaned on the island. "That's insane. I can't believe the police would think

Morgan had anything to do with Phil's death. There are plenty of people out there who had a much stronger reason to want that man dead."

I agreed wholeheartedly. "I think their suspicions regarding him will fade soon. My money's on Phil's wife. She not only lied to Detective Fiore about why she was at the office, she doesn't seem that upset—" I stopped and rolled my lips inward, realizing I'd just given away what else I'd been up to this morning.

Mom narrowed her eyes at me. "Delaney, what did you do? Did you go talk to Felicity?"

I shrugged slightly and glanced away. "Maybe," I muttered.

She sighed and pushed back from the counter, walking over to the dishes she'd recently washed, touching one. "You know, what they say about middle children is true. Recklessness is your middle name."

I couldn't help but smile. I might have been known to leap without thinking once or twice. "Where's the fun in life by thinking first?"

She looked over her shoulder at me, spearing me with an exasperated glare, before turning back to her dishes. They must have been dry, because she was busy stacking serving bowls.

"Anyway, I'm actually not here to spill the tea about what happened. I need a favor."

"What sort of favor?"

"Can I borrow the inn's van and a couple of collapsible tables? If my bakery truck isn't repaired by this afternoon, I mean."

"Oh. Of course. Do you think it'll be ready? Does Yves know what's wrong with it?"

"He said it might be the fuel pump. And he was hopeful he'd have it done this afternoon. I just want some contingency plans in place, you know? It'll be my luck the part will be back-ordered and won't be here for two weeks."

Chuckling, Mom picked up the pile of plates. "That's karma. Maybe you shouldn't stick your nose in other people's business."

I huffed. "It broke *before* I watched Mr. Brunswick career over the cliff, thank you."

Mom hummed. "Right, but you meddled before Yves started looking at the truck."

My mouth pulled. I still highly doubted karma or fate or whatever was at play here, but arguing wouldn't do me any good. She'd find some reason to say she was right. So, I stayed silent and hoped she'd change the subject.

Ceramic clinked as Mom put the dishes away. "So, you talked to Daphne, then? I suppose she told you her happy news?" Mom glanced back, smiling brightly.

Mentally, I swiped the sweat off my forehead. *Phew!* She let it go.

I smiled back. "She did, yes. We discussed it this morning, actually. She's thinking a deep crimson or a rich purple for bridesmaids' dresses and for the cake, which she asked me to make. With lighter accents. Gold, cream, green. That sort of thing. She might change her mind, though. I pulled out a bunch of different food colorings and told her to take a picture and do some research. She said she'd nail down a color scheme by the end of the weekend."

"Good. We need to get moving on this. I can't believe she wants to pull a wedding together in less than four months." She picked up her skillet, wiping it off with a clean towel. "I'm not sure she realizes just how much work it will be."

"I don't, either, but I can also understand not wanting to wait over a year. I mean, I know people do it all the time, but they usually want all the trappings, you know? She'll be happy with some chairs on the lawn, a few flower sprays, and a pretty dress, so it won't be quite so crazy."

Mom sighed. "I know. That's good, because that's all she's going to get. Have you thought about cake flavors?"

"Not really. She'll probably want something simple. Vanilla or maybe almond. Morgan might like something a little different, though. He's more adventurous. Maybe I'll sit them down Sunday evening and we'll discuss it."

"I think we should call a family meeting and have a group planning session."

"That's probably not a bad idea. This is going to be an all-hands-on-deck kind of affair."

"Exactly. I'll call her on her lunch break today and suggest that. We could probably discuss things at our weekly family lunch on Sunday. Did you eat breakfast?" she asked, changing the subject once more. "I have some food left if you're hungry."

"I ate a cinnamon roll. I'm good."

"You're sure?"

"Yes." I pushed away from the island and stood. "I need to get back to work. I'll let you know how things go with my truck later."

"Okay. Have a good day, sweetie."

"I will." Turning I headed for the door.

"And keep your nose out of Phil Brunswick's death."

Reaching the door, I tossed a sunny smile at her over my shoulder. "Bye, Mom." I knew myself. Mom was right; I'm nosy. So, I wasn't about to make a promise I couldn't keep.

"Delaney…" Her voice held a note of warning.

I waggled my fingers and opened the door. "See you later." Before she could say more, I ducked through into the garage and away from her knowing stare.

Eight

Bleary-eyed, I stared at the clock on my stainless-steel stove as I sipped my morning coffee the next day. I'd slept later than usual, thanks to yesterday's forced baking day. Mornings were always rough for me, but sleeping late was becoming a bit of a habit.

Millie hopped up onto the stool beside me and meowed. She bumped my arm with her soft head.

"Hi, sweet girl." I scratched her multi-colored head between her ears. "You want your breakfast?"

The cat meowed again.

I got up and went to the row of maple cupboards, extracting a can of cat food. Picking up Millie's dish from the floor, I opened the can and dumped it into the bowl, all to a chorus of excited meows.

"Okay. Here you go."

Millie jumped down from the stool and ran over to the placemat where I set her bowls. Bending down, I put the dish next to her water, smiling as she attacked it.

She'd done that since she was a kitten. Just dove straight in. Sometimes, she even made little noises while she ate, though she did that less now that she was older.

After refilling Millie's water, I finished my coffee, then made a cup to go and gathered up what I'd need for the day. Unfortunately, Yves hadn't been able to get the parts in for my truck yesterday. The bride and groom had okayed me setting up with tables, so I needed to pick up my parents' van and load all my wares.

Millie hopped up onto the stool again as I stuffed my sketchpad and my lunch into my tote. Lifting one paw, she licked it, then cleaned her face.

"Is your belly full now?" Giving my cat another scratch, I leaned in and kissed her head, then looped the handles of my bag over my shoulder. "I'll see you a little later, Mills. Hold down the fort."

Ignoring me, Millie went back to cleaning her face.

With a chuckle and an eye roll, I scooped up my keys from the white quartz counter. It was nice to know I'd be missed.

The first rays of sunshine were breaking the horizon as I pulled away from my little cream-colored cottage. As I wove through town and up the mountain to the inn, the golden glow intensified, lightening the sky and bathing the world in warmth. Dew sparkled on the pine boughs and dripped onto my windshield as I turned down the lane.

Entering the clearing near the house, I saw Dad set up with some sawhorses and several pine boards.

I parked near the van and got out.

"Morning, Laney." Dad lifted a gloved hand and waved. The light breeze ruffled his short salt and pepper hair.

Smiling, I walked over. "Morning. What are you making?" It was not unusual to find him tinkering first thing in the morning. He was an early riser and had probably been up a couple of hours already.

He glanced at the pile of boards, then back at me. "Your mom asked me to build her a bookshelf for her office. She's filled the one in the living room."

"Ah. I see. Why do you look perplexed, though? You built the other one without a problem."

His head bobbed. "I did. But she wants this one to go all the way to the ceiling and have a library ladder." He rolled his eyes, sighing. "The things we do for love."

I chuckled. "Well, I'd stay and offer to help, but I have a wedding to get ready for."

"Your mother said you wanted to borrow the van and some tables." He took off his eye protection and gloves, leaving them on a sawhorse. "Come on. I'll help you load up."

"You don't have to do that, Dad. I can handle it."

He offered me a wide smile. "It gives me a few more minutes to figure out how I'm going to build the railing for the ladder."

I laughed. "Doesn't it come as like a kit?"

His footsteps slowed and a frown wrinkled his brow. "They make library ladder kits?"

"Yes." I pulled out my phone. "Here. Look." Opening my internet browser, I ran a quick search, showing him.

"Well, I'll be. Send me that link, would you? I was going to build it out of some iron pipe, but that's even better."

Copying the link, I texted it to him. "I don't know how you'd survive without me, Dad."

Mouth tilting, he gave me a side-eyed glance. "I'm sure I'd find a way."

"Maybe. But you'd be a lot more stressed." Grinning, I spun on my heel and headed for the van to the sound of him huffing a laugh.

While I opened the van's rear doors and removed the few supplies stored inside, Dad brought the tables around from the storage shed and loaded them up. He also brought me a chair, for which I was immensely grateful. I wouldn't have remembered to grab a camp chair. It wasn't on my list.

Shutting the doors, I turned and gave him a hug. "Thanks for the help."

"Anytime. If you need more later, holler. I'll probably be ready for another break from this shelving unit."

I smiled, easing back and heading for the passenger door of my car to get my bag. "I'll keep that in mind." Retrieving my tote, I got in the van.

The engine roared to life with a quick flick of my wrist. Waving at Dad, I pulled away from the inn.

In all honesty, he was probably right. I should have hired an assistant for today. Weddings were always labor intensive. But for this one, I'd decided to save some money and do it solo. The bride and groom were doing a food truck rally, and my truck was providing dessert as well as a cupcake tower rather than a traditional tiered wedding cake. It was a lot of setup, but nothing that required two people to stack things.

But now that I had to arrange *all* my baked goods on tables and not just the cupcake tower, an extra set of hands would come in handy.

Too late now.

Sighing at my lack of forethought, I did my best not to worry about the work. It wouldn't change anything.

Instead, I ran through the list of things I needed to load into the van.

Eight dozen chocolate chip cookies.

Eight dozen frosted sugar cookies.

Four sheet pans of mini cinnamon rolls.

Five dozen fruit tartlets.

Eight dozen brownies.

Six dozen cake pops.

Twelve dozen cupcakes in two different flavors.

One eight-inch cake for the bride and groom to cut.

One six-inch anniversary cake for the bride and groom to take home and freeze.

And a hundred and thirty favor boxes filled with mini vanilla macarons.

I'd been working for weeks on this wedding. It had to go well, so the bride would recommend me to her friends. There were several of them engaged. Landing those contracts could put a huge dent in what I still needed to open my own shop.

Starting off without my food truck for a food truck rally wasn't ideal.

But I had a plan.

Before I bought my truck, I catered parties and attended every craft fair, bake sale, and farmer's market I could find. I still had all my display items from those. Today, my packrat tendencies would pay off.

The only items I was worried about were the fruit tartlets and the macarons. The tartlets not on display needed to stay refrigerated and would be hard to store. The macrons also needed to be refrigerated until I distributed them on the tables, but they would be easier to transport because I could stack them. I'd already planned to put those in some large styrofoam coolers with gel ice packs to keep them cool.

But I had a brainwave last night while I tried to fall asleep. I kept a large cooler in storage. If I filled the bottom with a couple of inches of ice, I could stack some baking racks inside with the tartlets. The church had a cooler I could borrow too. One way or another, I'd get them all to this wedding.

Back in town, I turned toward the storage facility where I rented a small unit to house my baking supplies. After loading up the cooler and some of the display items, I headed for the church.

The sun was burning bright by the time I pulled into the parking lot. Getting out, I locked the van, then let myself into the church. Before I could even think about loading up, I had to finish some of the desserts. Like the tartlets.

And the cupcakes.

And the cinnamon rolls.

At least the cookies, brownies, and cake pops were ready to go.

Flipping on the light, I hurried down the steps. In the kitchen, I set my tote down and opened the fridge to get the butter.

Time to get to work.

Nine

My stomach growled as I set out the last tray of cookies. Briefly, I debated snatching one, just to appease it, but resisted. I had a lunch in the van. One that would now be more like dinner, since I hadn't had time to eat yet.

It had taken me longer to layer the fruit on the tartlets than I thought it would. I couldn't just toss it all on and call it a day. If I wanted to make the best impression possible, it needed to look like I cared.

But I was done, and the tables looked amazing, even if they also looked out of place amongst the food trucks setting up shop around me.

Stepping back, I ran an assessing eye over my setup. Under a white canopy, I had three tables pushed together to form a flattened semicircle. Fern green tablecloths covered the tables—my signature color. On the center table, I'd draped a cream table runner over the center to hang down and show my logo. On each end of my display, I had dessert towers. One was stacked with brownies and the other I would load with tartlets just before the reception started. In between, I had gold platters laden with cinnamon rolls, cookies, and cake pops, some of them sitting atop small, overturned crates to give the display some depth. Woven between the platters were warm white fairy lights and flowers that matched the bride's bouquet. The wedding planner had given me some of the pale pink roses to use on the cake table, and I'd liked the aesthetic, so I ran out earlier and bought some extras to use on my dessert tables.

"Hey, this looks great."

I glanced to my left and saw Tyson approaching.

"Thanks." I offered him a sunny smile.

"I was a little worried when you said your truck was in the shop and you had to set up under a tent." He swirled a finger at my display. "But you've done a great job."

"I channeled my craft show days." I grinned.

"Well, you did good."

"Thanks."

"Do you need any help?"

I chewed on the corner of my lip. "Not with this, but if you have time, you could help me set up the cake table." It was the simplest of the displays, so I'd saved it for last.

"Sure." He swept out an arm. "Lead the way."

Walking around the tables, I opened the rear doors on the van and slid an eight-foot table free.

"I'll take that." Tyson took it from my hands.

I leaned in and lifted the tote with the cream tablecloth and copper-colored platters that matched the wedding color scheme. This part of the job had all been pre-planned since the cupcake tower was separate from the food truck rally.

Grabbing the last item I needed for the initial setup and decoration—the roses the wedding planner gave me—I tucked them under my arm and then shut the doors.

Tyson followed me across the parking lot to the grassy area where the event venue had set up rows of round tables for the guests. When the wedding planner brought me the flowers earlier, I asked her where she wanted me to set up the cake table, and she said off to the side, opposite the DJ. He was busy setting up the last of his speakers on the left side of the party area, near the dance floor, so I headed for the right side under a large maple tree. The shade would help keep the frosting from melting in the sun.

Setup went quickly with Tyson's help. I was grateful. The tummy grumbles were becoming louder and more frequent. I had enough time to spare to hide in the van for a few minutes and eat.

Peanut butter had never tasted so good.

Once I finished my meal, I grabbed a clean t-shirt with my logo on it and ducked inside the small cottage that served as a ready room for the wedding party and contained bathrooms for the guests. Changing out of my sweaty top, I fixed my ponytail and put on a modicum of makeup, then returned to my table.

Guests had begun to arrive and were staging near the small pond where the ceremony would take place.

The scent of barbecued meat and Mexican spices filled my nose as I reached my tent. Even though I'd just eaten, the thought of a burrito made my mouth water. If Tyson had any food left at the end of the night, I might have to see if he'd let me buy a grilled chicken burrito. That sounded fantastic.

While more people wandered in and headed down the lane to the ceremony site, I dug into the van for the last item on my to-do list: the mini macaron party favors. Luckily, they were light and the coolers I'd packed them into fit nicely on a hand truck. I could wheel it around the tables as I set a box out at each place setting.

Sliding the hand truck out from the van's side wall, I loaded the three styrofoam coolers onto it and headed for the dinner tables, pleased with myself.

So far, things were going off without a hitch.

Ten

W hat was *he* doing here?

I forced a smile onto my face and lifted a sugar cookie onto the maid-of-honor's plate, all while surreptitiously staring over her shoulder at the tall, dark-haired man in the charcoal suit and light blue dress shirt sipping from a champagne flute and speaking with the bride's father.

Detective Fiore looked even better dressed up than he did in the black tactical pants and polo shirt he'd worn to Phil Brunswick's accident scene.

A lot better.

Why did men in suits have to look so dang handsome?

Not that he wasn't, anyway.

He shifted his gaze, looking directly at me.

I quickly averted my eyes, concentrating on the line of people coming past my tables.

So what if he was here? It was obvious he was here as a guest and not in any official capacity. And despite his good looks distracting me, he was a reminder of an event I was trying to keep out of the forefront of my mind.

I'd been succeeding, too, enjoying myself and the happy

wedding guests. Now I had to fight the scowl that wanted to appear.

My gaze strayed to him again.

His flicked to me, then he excused himself from the bride's father.

Crap! He was coming this way.

Gritting my teeth, I focused on the line of people. I couldn't stop him if he wanted to get dessert. But I could hope he went away quickly.

He got in line, shuffling forward as people chose their desserts and walked away.

My teeth clenched a little harder with each step he took.

As the last person in front of him stepped up, I forced myself to take a deep breath and to relax. I didn't know why his presence had me so anxious.

Liar.

I glared at my inner voice, but knew she was right. My anxiety probably had something to do with the meddling I'd done yesterday. He wouldn't be happy to find out I'd spoken to Felicity Brunswick.

"Good evening, Ms. Fowler."

His low, rich voice rumbled over me, sending an electric current over my nerve endings. It shouldn't be possible for a simple sentence to cause such a reaction, but I couldn't deny the tingle humming through my body now.

I did my best to make my smile reach my eyes and not give away the nerves—the bad kind—churning in my stomach. "Good evening, Detective. Enjoying the festivities?"

He smiled, the relaxed expression so entirely different from what I saw of him the other night and yesterday morning that my brain short-circuited momentarily, and I missed what he said in reply.

Cheeks coloring, I blinked away the brain fog. "Sorry, I spaced out. It's been a long day. What did you say?"

His dark eyes took on an amused glint. "I said, yes, I am."

"Oh." I chuckled nervously. "Good."

His gaze wandered over the tables, then out to the crowd. "It's been nice getting to know a few more people in town."

"How long have you been here?" I knew he was a recent transplant, but not how recent.

"Just a few weeks. I started at the department in May."

"Ah. Is the bride or groom someone you work with?" That would explain why he was here.

Another thought struck me. One that made me a little uncomfortable, considering the way I'd been lusting after him in his suit. "Or did you come as someone's plus one?"

He smiled at me. "No. I'm alone. The groom is a friend from college. That's actually why I took the job here. When I was looking for a change, Grant mentioned there was an opening here for a detective. I applied and the rest is history."

"Oh. Well, that's nice. I'm glad it worked out for you."

"Me too." He gave me another quick smile, then looked at the tablescape again. "So, what's good?"

"All of it."

He laughed. "You're not modest."

Grinning, I shook my head. "No. Not when it comes to my baking."

"I already tried one of your macarons, so I can understand why. It was delicious."

My cheeks heated again at the compliment. "Thank you."

Nerves hitting me once more, I folded my hands together and looked down. "As for what you should try, I guess that depends on your preferences. The cake pops are the same cake as the cupcakes." I gestured to the cake table on the far side of the dining area. That had yet to be delved into. "If you like a more bright dessert, the fruit tartlet would be a good choice. There are also the fan favorite comfort desserts, the chocolate chip cookie and the brownie." I held a hand out toward each.

A wrinkle formed between his eyebrows. "What's in the fruit tartlet?"

I moved toward that end of the table. "It's a standard shortbread crust filled with a light lemon chiffon mousse and topped with fresh berries. I brought whipped cream, too, if you'd like to top it off."

He tipped his head. "That sounds good. Especially since I'll probably eat a cupcake a little later. I'll take the fruit tart."

Nodding once, I picked up a small plate off the stack and used a flat metal spatula to slide a tartlet off the tower and onto the plate.

"Did you want whipped cream?"

"No. It's fine like that."

I held the plate out to him. "There you go. Would you like anything else?"

"No, this is plenty. Thank you."

"You're welcome." Relaxing some, I gave him a more genuine smile. "Enjoy."

"I will." Raising his half-empty champagne glass in farewell, he walked away.

I drew in a deep breath, watching him for a moment, before turning to the next person in line.

I'd survived.

It wasn't long after Detective Fiore came through my line that the steady stream of people died down and everyone took their seats for more traditional reception festivities. I was even able to sneak into my van and eat a quick snack.

Toward the end of the evening, I began paring back the items on my tables. People had eaten their fill and only the occasional guest walked by and grabbed a cookie or a cake pop now. I didn't have too much left, but it was enough to fulfill the bride's wishes for the leftovers. Tomorrow morning, I was to take whatever didn't get eaten to a local nursing home. She'd also asked me to bake a batch of carrot cake cupcakes to take to them in honor of her grandmother who'd passed away a month after she got engaged. The nursing home was the one where the woman had lived until she passed.

I was so touched by the gesture I only charged her for the ingredients for the carrot cake and not my time to make the cupcakes.

"Packing up?"

I spun around at the male voice, startled. Most people in the last hour had just grabbed what they wanted without a word.

"Sorry. Didn't mean to startle you." Detective Fiore held up a hand.

I smiled. "That's all right. I was in my own little world. Did you come back for seconds?"

"Actually, I just came to say goodnight and to tell you that your cupcakes and the fruit tartlet were fantastic. I've eaten more sweets tonight than I have all month."

I blinked, not sure I heard him correctly. "You had what? Three, four things tonight?"

He nodded.

"And that's more than you ate all month?"

He shrugged. "I'm not a big sweet eater. Usually." He chuckled at the wide-eyed look I gave him. "You look like I told you my favorite food is crickets."

My nose wrinkled. Gross. "That's just unfathomable to me. I know I probably shouldn't, but I eat at least a piece of chocolate every day." I crossed my arms, shifting to cock one hip out as I stared at him. "Seriously, though, how do you live like that?"

He laughed. "Quite easily. Though knowing I now live in a town where I can get such delicious treats, I might find it a little more difficult."

Warmth sprang to life in my chest at the compliment. "Thank you."

Rapping his knuckles on the table softly, he took a step

back. "Anyway, I just wanted to tell you that. Have a good night, Ms. Fowler."

"I—"

The rest of what I was about to say got drowned out by a loud crash.

Detective Fiore spun around to face the sound. I peered around him at the dining area, where all I could see were two pairs of male feet flailing in the air amidst a collapsed table.

"What in the world?" I muttered.

The detective took off running toward the fray.

Shouts and exclamations of surprise filled the air as the two men continued to fight, even as the tablecloth and all the tableware fell on top of them. I moved around to the front of my tent to get a better view, but stayed back. There was nothing I could do by going over there, and I didn't want to get in the way.

"Hey!" Detective Fiore reached the fracas. He extended an arm and grabbed the man on top. "That's enough."

A groomsman appeared, and with his help, they pulled the man off the one he was attempting to beat to a pulp.

"Lemme go!"

Even from here, I could see the rage on the man's face. I didn't recognize him or the man Tyson and another man were helping to his feet.

"No. You need to calm down." Detective Fiore hooked an arm around the man's, keeping him from lunging at the victim again.

The guy jerked in the detective's hold, eyes locked on the other man. I watched as the victim glared back and dabbed at his bleeding face.

"You d'serve so mush more than a bloody nose for tha' comment," the angry man slurred. "How dare you insin-yate such a thing! She would never!" He jerked against Detective Fiore again.

Detective Fiore jerked him back. "Enough!" He turned to

the victim. "Go inside the cottage. I'll deal with you in a moment."

The victim turned his glare on him. "Who the hell are you to tell me what to do?"

I rolled my lips in and raised my eyebrows. That guy had a lot of nerve. Perhaps aided by a few too many glasses of champagne, like his friend?

"Detective Fiore, Carter County Sheriff's Department." He paused for a second, letting that information sink in. "Now go inside, please."

The man stared at Detective Fiore for several moments before turning toward the cottage. Cream linen tangled around his shoes, and he stumbled.

Tyson reached out to catch him, but he pushed him away. "Don't touch me!"

Immediately, Tyson held up his hands. I heard him say something but was too far away to make out what. The man regained his balance and stomped away.

Curiosity got the better of me, and I moved closer.

"—your name?" As I moved in, I caught the tail end of Detective Fiore's question.

"Nate."

"Okay, Nate. How about you tell me what's going on?"

"Ask Bryant," the man spat.

"I will. But right now, I'm asking you. Why'd you tackle him into the table?"

Nate huffed, glancing away. "He said... he insin-yated that my wife was hav-having an affair with Phil Brunswick. And that now that he's dead, maybe she'd like to come warm his bed." Having put a little more effort into speaking, his words were less slurred this time.

My eyes widened. Who would say such a thing? Especially to someone's husband? Bryant had to be as drunk as this guy. It was the only explanation I could come up with for such behavior. Normal people didn't behave that way.

"Okay. I get why you're upset. But we can't be slinging people into dinner tables at weddings."

Nate turned his head, glaring at Detective Fiore. "I di'n sling him. I tackled him."

"Right." Detective Fiore sighed. "Come on. Let's go find you a seat."

"Don' wanna sit." Nate stumbled as the detective propelled him forward.

"Tough." Detective Fiore forced him into a chair several feet away. "Where's your wife? Is she here?" He glanced around.

My gaze scanned the crowd as well, but I didn't see a woman who looked overly concerned—or pissed.

"No. She—" he broke off with a hiccup. After swallowing, he continued. "She's been workin' hard. At the law office. Said she was too tired tonight to come."

Detective Fiore's gaze sharpened. "What's your wife's name?"

Nate blinked up at him, resignation now settling onto his face. "Mandi."

My mouth dropped open a fraction. Mandi? As in blonde bombshell, supermodel Mandi? She was married to this guy?

I tipped my head, studying him. He wasn't unattractive. Take away the splotchy red, alcohol flush from his cheeks and the bloodshot eyes, and he'd be decently handsome. He was on the taller side and built like someone who'd probably played high school—maybe college—football, but had fallen out of the habit of daily exercise and let that middle-age paunch grow.

Still, they seemed like a rather mismatched couple.

"All right. I have more questions, but they need to wait. You sit tight here while I go talk to your buddy."

The resignation on Nate's face morphed into anger again. He surged out of his chair. "Don' call him that! He's not my friend!"

Detective Fiore grabbed his arm and pushed him back into the chair. "My apologies. Now, can you stay seated, or do I need to tie you to the chair?"

Belligerence brought Nate's eyebrows together. "Why you wanna restrain me? Go cuff that piece of—"

"All right, that answers that," Detective Fiore said, cutting him off. He tugged Nate from the chair, quickly getting behind him to thread a hand under his arm, then back over the man's shoulder to press against his neck.

"Hey!" Nate bent forward from the pressure. "What d'you think y're doin'?"

Detective Fiore didn't answer, just marched him toward the parking lot.

I ran after him. "Do you need some tape or something?" I asked, catching up. "I have a roll." I brought duct tape to tack down my tablecloths.

He glanced back at me. "Thank you, but no."

I debated going to get it, anyway, but decided—as a cop— he likely had everything in hand and hung back while they continued toward a dark blue pickup.

Reaching the truck, Detective Fiore pressed Nate up against the rear door, then dug into his pocket. A moment later, the truck beeped and the lights flashed as he unlocked it. Easing back a bit, he opened the passenger door and leaned in.

A second later, Nate lurched violently to his right, knocking the detective into the door.

"Oh!" A sharp gasp flew from my lips as Detective Fiore crashed into the window, then fell.

Stumbling around the rear of the truck, Nate took off.

My feet were moving before I realized it.

Dashing between two cars, I hurried forward to the next row. As I reached the rear of a full-size white SUV, Nate approached. I stuck my foot out past the car's bumper as he lurched past, tripping him.

With a shout of surprise, he fell forward, crashing into the gravel.

Seconds later, Detective Fiore ran up and pounced onto Nate's back. He had handcuffs clenched in his fist. In a couple of quick clicks, they were locked around the drunk man's wrists.

"Oh, c'mon, man! I di'n mean an'thing by that. It was a reflex."

"Uh-huh." The detective stood up, hauling Nate with him. "Sure."

Dark brown eyes met mine. "Thanks for the assist, Ms. Fowler."

I nodded. "You're welcome."

Eleven

"Selection is a little slim this morning, Delaney. I'm missing my raspberry danish."

I gave blue-haired Mrs. Albright a bright smile, even though I wanted to roll my eyes and tell her to be satisfied with what we had. After the chaos of yesterday evening, most of my prep time for the Sunday morning service was gone. She was lucky to have anything.

"I'm sorry. They'll be back next week." Mentally, I crossed my fingers, hoping I wasn't lying. The last few days had been a little on the crazy side, so I hoped that didn't continue.

The old woman hummed and moved on, lifting her sugar cookie to her bright pink lips to take a bite.

As soon as she turned away, I let my smile fall. Normally, I didn't mind manning the coffee counter at church. It was one of the best ways to stay caught up on the happenings around town. People loved to sit and gossip before the service started. I'd learned many things about the town's fine citizens since entering into this arrangement with the church.

A yawn stole over my face, and I covered it with my hand.

But today, I would have much preferred to sleep in.

"Big night?"

Blinking away the moisture in my eyes, I glanced over at Morris Beach. This time, I didn't bother to force a smile. I left it packed away altogether.

"Just busy." I picked up my tongs. "What can I get you this morning, Morris?"

The skin around his mud-colored eyes crinkled as he offered me a bright smile. The tilt to his head and the quick glance he ran over my body told me he was up to his old tricks, and I was about to be asked on a date once again.

I couldn't help myself and wrinkled my nose. At two years older than Daphne, Morris had decided it was past time he found a wife. Unfortunately, he'd set his sights on me. It wasn't that he was a bad guy. In fact, when he wasn't following me around, lowering himself to the level of street urchin as he begged me to go on a date, he could be quite interesting to talk to. But the flagrant refusal to take no for an answer after the millionth time I'd turned him down did not appeal to me.

He didn't notice my annoyance. With one last once over of my attire, he dropped his gaze to the selection of baked goods I'd laid out for the congregation this morning.

"I'll take a cinnamon roll. No one makes a cinnamon roll quite like you."

Offering him a tight smile, I lifted one onto a napkin. "Thank you."

"Wouldn't you like to be able to make these for your family?"

I frowned. "What do you mean? I do."

"Not your parents and your sisters. Your *own* family. A husband and children."

I scowled. "Morris, we've had this discussion. I am no more interested in marrying you now than the first time you asked. Why don't you go talk to Carol Prosser?" I tipped my chin toward the mousy woman standing near the coat rack with her mother.

He glanced Carol's way, thoughtfulness crossing his expression for a brief second before he turned back to me. "Mrs. Prosser would never allow it."

I arched an eyebrow. Lucile Prosser had been trying to marry her daughter off for longer than Morris had been chasing me. No one wanted to deal with the overbearing woman long enough, though, to get close to Carol. Which was a shame. She was a nice woman. "Have you asked?"

"Well… no."

"You should." I picked up a second cinnamon roll, placing it on a napkin, and handed it to him. "Take this to her. Carol, I mean. Not Lucile." I don't know why I didn't think of this before. They were perfect for each other. Morris wanted a woman he could "take care of." Carol was the type to appreciate that. She'd been sheltered her entire life. She was twenty-seven years old and still lived at home. The woman didn't even work because her mother wouldn't allow it.

But I knew Carol from the charity events we did together for the church. She had a backbone, but it was well hidden. I had a feeling Morris would be enamored enough with having a wife who fit his ideal of what a woman should be that he'd bend over backward to make her happy. In a relationship like that, and free of her mother's thumb, Carol would be able to stretch her independence.

I just hoped Lucile wouldn't stand in the way. Morris wasn't exactly the catch she'd hoped to get for Carol.

Sure, he was gainfully employed as a harvest manager for a local logging company, but Lucile wanted to see her daughter married to a doctor or a lawyer. There weren't many of them around here, though, and they were either already taken, or unwilling to put up with Lucile.

Morris might be just the man to be unbothered by her abrasive nature.

"You think she'd appreciate it?" He shifted, turning to stare at the woman.

"I do. Just make sure you don't let her mother run you off. Let Carol decide. And just a hint, she likes to walk in the forest and bird watch."

His brown eyes lit up. "Really?"

I nodded, biting back a smug smile. Morris liked to bird watch too. Once, he told me one of his favorite parts of his job was being on-site in the office trailer and watching the birds first thing in the morning. He also said the reason he took the job with the company was because they practiced sustainable logging. They didn't go in and clear-cut. Instead, they cleared deadfall or thinned out areas to decrease the fire danger.

It really was a shame he wanted a wife who didn't want to work outside the home. He was an interesting fellow.

Morris backed away from the counter, his expression thoughtful and now determined. "Thanks for the tip, Delaney."

I let my smile loose. "You're welcome."

Shaking my head at my own genius—and at how easy that was—I turned my attention to the cinnamon roll pan, covering it up so they didn't dry out.

"So you're playing matchmaker now?"

The deep voice that haunted my dreams last night filled my ears. I looked up and straight into Detective Fiore's rich brown eyes. A smile played with his sculpted lips.

My heart flip-flopped in my chest.

Why did he have to be so good looking?

To counter the flutters going on in my belly, I narrowed my eyes and tossed a question back at him. "Are you following me?"

He chuckled. "It would seem that way, wouldn't it?"

I hummed.

"I assure you, I'm not. I've been on a quest to find a church since I moved here. It's an important decision, so I've been spending a few weeks at different non-denominational ones and comparing the fit. This is my first week here."

"Oh?" Curiosity piqued, I relaxed a bit. "What do you think of us so far?"

He shrugged. "I only just got here. Though, I like the idea of the social time before the service." He turned, leaning against the counter to look out over the church members gathered in the lobby. "It encourages people to get to know each other."

"It does," I agreed.

He glanced at me, then back out at the crowd. "I'm sure there's a downside too. Like feeding gossip."

It was my turn to shrug. "Maybe some. But I've seen the gossip work in positive ways."

Detective Fiore raised an eyebrow. "How so?"

"Like when someone is in need, but doesn't want to ask for help. We had a family a year or so ago who'd fallen on hard times. The husband got hurt on the job and short-term disability only covered part of his salary. His wife was salaried at her job, so she couldn't pick up overtime. She also couldn't take on a second job because they have three kids she needed to be there for. Someone mentioned how their son was giving half their lunch, plus some extra stuff he was sneaking into his backpack, to the couple's oldest child for him to take home. Carol"—I nodded to Carol Prosser, who I was happy to see was talking to Morris—"overheard and said something to Maggie Smythe." I tipped my chin toward a woman near my mom's age, talking with the pastor. "The two of them put together a meal train for the family that got them through the two months until the husband could finally get back to work."

"Hey, that's great." The detective smiled.

"It is. So, see? Not all gossip is bad."

"No. It can definitely be helpful." His gaze turned pointed.

A pit formed in my stomach. His next words turned it into a ball.

"I heard you did some visiting the other day."

I glanced down briefly, my fingers fiddling with the foil covering the cinnamon rolls. "I visit a lot of people."

He propped his elbows on the counter and leaned in. "I bet you do. But I'm talking about someone in particular. Mrs. Brunswick?"

I smoothed a wrinkle in the foil. "I might have taken some baked goods to her house and offered my condolences. Who told you that?" I wanted to know so I could make sure to avoid that person in the future.

"Mrs. Brunswick."

"Oh." Well, avoiding her wouldn't be a problem. I didn't have a reason, really, to talk to her again.

"Yes. I asked her to keep a log of people paying their respects. When I spoke to her last night about Mandi Davis, I took a quick look at the list. Your name was on it."

"That shouldn't surprise you. Why wouldn't I pay my respects? I tried to save the man."

"Right, but most people have just called. You somehow worked your way past the main gate and into the house."

"His sister let me in. And speaking of her, did you know she and Felicity don't like each other very much? As I left, they practically came to blows. Felicity smacked her, and Skyler shoved her back."

His expression shifted, going from a smug surety to intent police officer. "Why were they fighting?"

"I'm not sure. When I got there, Skyler said her sister-in-law wasn't accepting visitors. She and I spoke for several minutes before Felicity came into the room. When she did, she wasn't very happy I was there, even after discovering who I was. She bordered on rude, really, and basically told me and Skyler to leave." I held up my hands. "I didn't stick around after that and only saw the argument through the window as I got into my car."

Detective Fiore's brows knit together. "Back up. What else was said while you were there?"

I drew in a breath and glanced past him, silently wishing someone else would come up in search of breakfast. But it was nearly time for the service to start, so most everyone had food who wanted it. I was stuck in this conversation for now.

"Felicity was upset when she came in that someone was there, since she'd asked not to be disturbed. I received a rude hello once she discovered who I was. Then she told me she didn't eat sugar or flour when I offered her one of the baked goods I brought. I told Skyler that was more for her, and she mentioned her sons would like it." I paused, frowning as I remembered Felicity's expression when that was said.

"What? What did you remember?"

"I don't know if it's anything. She—Felicity—kind of… sneered? When Skyler mentioned her kids." I thought about what else was said after that. "She also seemed to dislike her stepson, James."

"Phil's son?"

I nodded.

"What makes you think that?"

I lifted a shoulder. "Just the expression on her face. After Felicity asked to be left alone, Skyler mentioned the funeral planning that still needed to be done. Felicity sort of waved it away, saying it was James's problem since he was the estate's executor."

The detective rolled his lips inward, glancing away briefly before nodding. "Okay. Is there anything else you remember?"

"No. I didn't really stick around. Just long enough to understand neither woman really liked the other. And that Felicity didn't seem too heartbroken over her husband's death." It was true. She'd been more defensive than sad.

Music erupted from the sanctuary, signaling it was time for everyone to take their seats.

"Is there anything else you'd like to know, Detective?" I pushed away from the counter, untying the apron I wore to protect my dress.

"I think that's all for now." He took a step back, then stopped, raising a finger. "Just one thing, though."

The pit formed in my stomach again. Here it was. The warning to stay out of things or next time he wouldn't be so nice about it.

"Call me Jack."

I frowned and blinked several times, confused. "I'm sorry?" I said, not understanding.

"You called me 'Detective.' My name is Jack."

"Oh." My frown smoothed out for a moment, then returned as another thought occurred. "You don't want me addressing you by your title?"

"Not here. I'm just another person, seeking some spiritual growth."

"Mmm-hmm. That's why you asked me a bunch of questions about your case." A smile tipped one side of my mouth as I came around the breakfast counter.

He grinned. The dimples forming on his face prompted a return of the flutters in my chest.

"See? I told you I need to work on my personal growth."

A chuckle slid past my lips. "Smooth answer."

Still smiling, he offered me an arm. "Would you be so kind as to join me for the service?"

The smile fell off my face as a wide-eyed stare took over. "Oh. Um, well, I usually sit with my family."

Some of the light left his eyes. He slowly lowered his arm. "Right." He cleared his throat. "Of course. I'm sorry. I—"

"Come sit with us." The words popped free of their own volition. I didn't regret them, though. He looked a bit like a little boy who'd been told he couldn't play when I said I usually sat with my family. I refused to let him feel left out. Even if I was a bit worried I'd face another interrogation.

"Oh. That's all right. You don't need to invite me to sit with you. I'll just find a place in the back."

I snaked my arm through his and tugged. "Don't be ridiculous. You're sitting with us." Not waiting for him to respond, I walked toward the sanctuary doors.

He didn't resist.

Leading him up the aisle, I found the pew my family usually occupied. Darcy was already there, eyes on the program in her hand that rested atop her crossed legs. The flowy and colorful blue fabric floated around her legs as she kicked her foot.

"Hey, Darce." I slid into the pew. *Jack* sat down beside me.

Darcy glance up, her relaxed expression turning to one of surprise as she saw my companion. "Well, hello." Her gaze traveled over his long form, which was cloaked in a suit similar to the one he wore to the wedding last night.

She held out a hand. "I'm Darcy, Delaney's younger sister."

He clasped her fingers for a brief moment. "Jack Fiore."

The smile on Darcy's face disappeared, and she snatched her hand back. "As in Detective Fiore?"

I groaned. She'd been talking to Daphne.

Jack's forehead wrinkled with a frown. "Yes."

Darcy crossed her arms, turning her glare on me. "I cannot believe you'd invite *him* to sit with us. After the way he—he—interrogated! Morgan."

I sighed. "Darcy…"

Jack held up a hand. "It's all right," he said, looking at me before turning his attention to Darcy. "I understand where you're coming from. Just know there was nothing personal to the talk Morgan and I had. I was simply doing my job and trying to find Phil Brunswick's killer."

"Well, my sister's fiancé is not it," Darcy shot back.

"And if the evidence tells us that, then that's great."

I sat up as the meaning behind his words registered.

"What do you me, 'if?' We just had an entire discussion about how Felicity acted the morning after she found out her husband had been murdered. Why is Morgan even still on your list?"

"Because Mrs. Brunswick's attitude has nothing to do with how innocent or guilty Morgan Dean is. I have many suspects in this case, and I will work through them and mark them off my list. I will grant you that Morgan is low on the list, but he's not off of it yet."

I mimicked Darcy's pose and crossed my arms, now regretting trying to make nice with him.

Jack sighed. "I should have just sat in the back," he muttered.

I pressed my lips together, stopping myself from telling him to do that now. Kicking him out of the pew wasn't very kind. I could suck it up and sit beside him for the service.

"Good morning."

Glancing over, I saw my mother's smiling face as she stopped at the family pew. Her curious gaze landed on Jack, then on me. Dad had a similar expression on his face.

"Hi, Mom. Morning, Dad."

"Who's your friend?" Mom asked, sitting down. Dad slid in beside her.

"Delaney, the traitor, invited the enemy into our midst," Darcy said.

"He's new here." Rolling my eyes, I leveled a glare on my sister, silently telling her to stuff it, then looked at Mom. "This is Detective Fiore."

"Oh." Mom blinked.

Dad sighed.

Sheesh. Was no one on my side?

Reaching over Mom, Dad offered Jack a hand. "I'm Don. This is my wife, Danielle. Welcome. And I do mean that. But I'm afraid you'll get the cold shoulder from my youngest and my oldest. Darcy has always had a bit of a quick temper, and well, Daphne—" he stopped, arching an eyebrow. "You understand."

Jack shook Dad's hand. "I do. And that's okay. I have thick skin. Call me Jack, please."

"Jack." Dad gave his hand one more quick shake, then let go. "You'll need it."

"Good morn—What? No. Why is he sitting here?"

At the sound of Daphne's voice, we all turned. She stared daggers at Jack.

I saw the slightest slump to his shoulders. It couldn't be easy having people dislike you for your job all the time.

Something in me woke up, and I spoke before anyone else could. "Can it, Daph. He's not here to harangue anyone. Sit down and enjoy the service."

For a moment, I thought she'd ignore me and either lay into him—and me—or go sit somewhere else, but Morgan nudged her from behind.

"Sit. It's fine," he said.

From the slight divot between his dark brows, I could tell Jack's presence bothered him some, but he wasn't as irate as his fiancée.

"For what it's worth, I'm here for church and nothing more," Jack said.

Morgan met his gaze, holding it for a long moment, but said nothing.

Luckily, we were all saved from talking as the music swelled and the pastor stepped up to the pulpit. When he called for the first song and we stood, Daphne leaned back, glancing behind Jack to level another fierce glare on me.

I stifled a sigh. Maybe I could make up a last-minute catering job and get out of Sunday lunch.

Twelve

"What were you thinking?" Daphne got up from her seat at the long table and stomped toward me as I entered the family unit at the inn.

While I'd been able to hurry out of church after the service, claiming an urgent need to use the restroom, I hadn't been able to beg off lunch. Mom texted me on my way home, basically demanding I show up. We had a wedding to plan, she said.

At least I was comfortable for this discussion. I'd changed out of my skirt and blouse and into shorts and a t-shirt. And my favorite hiking sandals. If things got too rough, I'd grab a kayak and go out on the lake. I probably would anyway. It was a nice day for it, and I'd had little downtime lately.

I rolled my eyes and didn't even pretend to not know what she was talking about. "He was there alone, and it was his first time at the church. He's new to the area. I was just trying to be friendly and make him feel welcome."

"Babe, just let it go," Morgan spoke up from the table. "I'm really not that big of a suspect. Detective Fiore was just doing his job."

"She still should have had your back." Her brows descended into a deep vee as she stared at me.

I propped my hands on my hips, meeting her glare. "I do. And if I genuinely thought having him in our midst would have caused more problems for Morgan, I wouldn't have invited him to sit with us."

"Enough, girls," Dad said, coming in the room, carrying a stock pot with steam wafting from the top. "Daphne, it's fine. We all know you're just upset still because he suspected Morgan of wrongdoing at all. Leave your sister alone. She was being nice." He set the pot on the trivet in the center of the table.

Daphne huffed, but some of the fight went out of her, loosening her shoulders. Spinning on her heel, she marched back to the table and sank into her seat beside her fiancé.

I walked forward more slowly and took a seat at the end and not directly across from her. Mom came in the room with a basket of bread in one hand and a bowl of salad in the other.

"Are we good?" she asked. "Can we eat in peace?"

"Yes," Daphne muttered.

I smiled and nodded, having no desire to argue with anyone.

"Good." Mom sat down. "Dig in."

Plates were lifted and filled from the pot of spaghetti Dad brought in, and soon, the earlier tiff was forgotten. Conversation flowed around the table and touched on many things—except Phil Brunswick's death, which was fine by me. I didn't want him bringing down what was usually a fun and relaxing afternoon tradition for our family.

Once everyone had eaten enough to appease their hunger, Mom brought up the wedding.

"Have you nailed down a color scheme, Daphne?"

Sharing a look with Morgan, Daphne slowly nodded. "I think so." She glanced at me. "We're going with the colors you suggested. The crimson with gold, pale green, and cream accents."

"I think that'll look great," I said. "Are we wearing burgundy dresses?"

Daphne nodded. "I found a style online I think will look good on everyone. We can get it locally. I checked. The lady I talked to said if we come this week, the dresses would arrive with a couple weeks to spare."

"I'm free any evening," Darcy said.

"I can come tomorrow or Wednesday," I said.

Daphne nodded. "Let's do Wednesday. They're open late that day. That will give me time to get measurements from Natasha and Aislyn," she said, mentioning two of her friends who lived out of town.

"Perfect. There's one thing off the list," Mom said. "What about your guest list? We can accommodate a hundred or so guests here. I'm glad you were willing to compromise on the day. October is still wedding season, so having yours on a Sunday made things much easier. It'll be a busy weekend, but at least it's spread out now."

"We're working on it," Morgan said. He wiped his mouth with a black linen napkin, then set it down on top of his empty plate.

"Good. The sooner the better. We need to get the invitations printed and sent." Mom smiled. "I've already talked to the print shop in town. Craig gave me some samples." She pushed away from the table. "Hang on. Let me get them. They're upstairs."

While Mom left the room, the rest of us finished our meals. We were gathering dishes when she returned. I picked up Daphne's and Morgan's plates so they had room to spread things out. When I returned, they had ten different types and colors of cardstock on the table in front of them. Mom held another piece with different fonts embossed on it in gold.

I held up my hands. "This looks like a you thing." I

pointed at my sister. "I was just here to find out the color scheme and what dress I need to wear."

She chuckled. "Chicken. Fine. Leave us." Making a shooing motion, she stuck her nose in the air.

I laughed. "I will."

"Wait for me." Darcy got up.

"I'm going out on the lake."

"Even better."

I eyed her skirt and high-heeled sandals with a skeptical arch of my eyebrow.

She chuckled. "I have clothes in the car."

"Well, go change then."

"That's the plan." Darcy rolled her eyes at me and followed me to the door.

"I'll go pull the boats while you get ready." I pointed toward the rack of kayaks and canoes near the shore.

"Sounds good. Thanks."

With a nod, I walked away.

Humming to myself, I lifted two bright blue kayaks off the racks and towed them down the grassy slope to the shoreline.

Anticipation tickled my senses. It had been far too long since I'd been on the water. Lately, my bakery business had eaten up every waking minute of my time. But with that wedding out of the way, I had a bit of a breather. I still had my normal food truck route and a few catering jobs lined up, but my next large event was the Fourth of July festival in two weeks. That was just regular desserts, though. Nothing terribly elaborate, just a lot of baking.

And speaking of elaborate, I probably should have asked Daphne and Morgan what flavors they wanted. We had time, though. I needed to mockup a few designs, anyway. We could talk flavors then.

Retreating to the boat rack, I ducked underneath to the large, long box we kept there that housed the paddles and life vests. Getting one of each for myself and Darcy, I reemerged to see her walking toward me.

"That was quick." I paused, waiting for her.

"I didn't want to get roped into giving my opinion. Mom had her laptop out and was listing off types of flowers."

I chuckled. "Remind me to elope when I get married."

Darcy laughed. "Same."

After gearing up, we dragged the boats into the water and climbed in, pushing away from shore.

"Where do you want to go?" Darcy dipped an oar in the water and glanced my way.

Fernwood Lake was the result of a dam downriver. When the dam flooded the area back in the sixties, it followed the natural terrain of the valley and created several forks. The inn was on the main body of the lake.

"We could paddle up to the western fork. Go look at all the fancy houses. We haven't done that in a while."

Darcy nodded once. "Works for me."

Picking up our pace, we headed out into the lake.

Today, it was an easy glide. There was little wind, so the water was like glass, and we cut through it with ease.

Conversation flowed much the same way. Darcy and I had both been so busy we'd seen little of each other for the last couple of weeks. Just on Sundays after church. And even then, I'd jetted off right after we ate to work. But with the wedding over, I could relax this week.

It was sorely needed.

With every stroke of my paddle through the water, I felt a little more of the stress tightening my shoulders ebb. The truck, the shock from watching Phil Brunswick die, work—it all melted away.

"So, why did you really invite Detective Fiore to sit with us?"

Darcy's question brought some of the tension back. I

inhaled a deep breath and forced it to leave. The invitation really wasn't a big deal.

"For the reasons I stated. He was new there and didn't really know anyone."

"So, Christian duty?" She smirked.

I glared at her. "I hate that phrase. And no. I was just being nice. He's not an ogre, you know. Just a man trying to do his job."

Darcy's smile dimmed. "Maybe so, but he still tried to pin a murder on Morgan."

"He did not." I sighed. "He questioned him because Morgan argued with Phil the day he died and Morgan's wallet was in Phil's car. He's talked to other people too. Trust me, Morgan isn't the only one on the suspect list."

"Ha!" Darcy pointed a finger at me. "So you admit he's on the list."

"Of course he is. They argued and the wallet places him in the car. Morgan also doesn't really have an alibi, and Jack hasn't figured out a motive yet."

"Jack? We're on a first name basis with the detective?" Darcy's gaze sharpened. "Is there something going on with you two?"

My face heated. I glanced up at the sky, exasperated, and hoped I could convince her the sudden redness was from the sun. "No."

Darcy hummed. "Sure." A grin broke out on her pretty face. "You know, it's okay if you're attracted to him. He's not hard to look at. And you haven't had a date in, well, forever."

"I'm busy." Which was true. I didn't have time for a relationship.

"That's bull. If you found someone you really liked, you could make time. I think you're scared."

"Scared?" I looked at her with a sharp turn of my head. "Of what?"

"Commitment. Being vulnerable."

"Says the woman who's also not involved with anyone." I gave her a pointed look.

Darcy waved a hand. "We're not talking about me. But"—she held up a finger—"if we were, I'm younger than you and not ready to settle down."

"Who says I am?"

"Please. You're thirty."

She looked at me like I was ancient, and I laughed. "You're twenty-seven, dear sister. Not that far behind."

"But I am behind." She gave me a smug look and tipped a finger at me. "Anyway, I think you should take a chance. If not with the gorgeous detective, then what about Tyson?"

I frowned, and my paddling slowed. "Tyson? Harris?" What was with my sisters wanting me to date him?

Darcy nodded. "He's good looking. And he's nice. Plus, you guys have the whole food truck business in common." Her expression brightened. "You could combine your efforts with a truck called Baked Goods and Burritos."

My nose wrinkled. "Those two things don't go together."

A wicked smile crossed Darcy's face. "They do if you're stoned and have the munchies."

Laughing, I shook my head and picked up speed again. "That's a limited clientele. I think we're good the way we are."

She shrugged. "Suit yourself. But you could still have a relationship with him. I know he likes you."

A crease formed between my eyebrows. "You think?" He'd never asked me out, but he did go out of his way to talk to me sometimes. Honestly, I never paid that much attention. I was always at the rallies to work, not socialize.

"Please." Darcy rolled her eyes. "I've seen the way he looks at you. His gaze follows you around like a lost puppy. I just think he's too shy to ask you out. You should ask him."

"I don't know, Darce. He's a friend."

"So? Wouldn't it be better to be with someone you know

you like and have stuff in common with? Instead of guessing if you might hit it off?" Water trickled off her paddle as she raised one end to dip the other into the lake.

"Maybe. I guess so." My frown intensified. "I don't know." I sighed. "I'm still too busy to date, so it doesn't matter."

Darcy groaned. "One day, you'll decide to stop hiding behind your business and want a personal life, but he—and all the other good men your age—will be taken."

It was my turn to roll my eyes. Darcy was ever the drama queen. "I'm sure there will be someone out there still."

"Oh, sure. But it'll be people like Morris Beach."

My mind flashed to church this morning. I doubted even Morris would be available soon.

Maybe Darcy was right, and I should start paying more attention to my dating life. While I definitely wasn't ready to settle down now, I could try a casual relationship. If it had potential to turn into more, well, then I could revisit my priorities.

"I got you thinking, didn't I?" She waggled a finger at me.

My mouth flattened, and I looked at her askance. "Maybe."

She grinned.

Not wanting to continue with her interrogation, I picked up my pace. "Race you to White Pine Point!"

"What? Hey! No fair!"

I heard a bit of frantic splashing as she sped up, before she settled into the new rhythm, and laughed.

But I didn't slow down. Even when my arm muscles burned, I kept my faster pace. I'd probably pay for it later with sore shoulders, but I didn't care. This was something I hadn't done in a while, and it was exhilarating.

Finally, we rounded the point into the western fork. Darcy sat back with a groan, letting her kayak glide.

"I hate you. Why did you make me do that?"

I chuckled and glanced over, gliding along beside her. "Because it felt good and was fun."

"It was neither of those things."

"You could have kept your slower pace."

"And let you win?" She gave me a dirty look. "Pfft, no."

"What are you talking about? I still won."

"But I didn't let you win." She tipped a finger toward me. "You're just faster. I blame it on all the cake decorating you do. Your arms are used to the work."

"They're used to being raised without support. Not flinging a paddle back and forth." I raised the oar and gave it a shake.

Darcy waved a hand. "Semantics."

I huffed out a breath. "You're impossible." Chuckling, I dipped my paddle in the water and set off again.

For another ten minutes, we paddled and chitchatted, trading barbs and laughter. As we kayaked deeper into the fork, the homes on the banks grew larger. Mom and Dad's inn wasn't small, but it could fit in the garage of some of these places. A lot of them were vacation homes for people from Seattle. When they wanted to get away from the hustle and bustle of city life, they'd make the drive out here. Or fly. Many of them took private jets into our tiny airport and just kept cars here. Soon, many of the homes would be occupied for the upcoming holiday. We'd picked a good day to go out on the lake. The boat traffic was low. It wouldn't be that way in a couple of weeks. The Fourth of July was a huge holiday around here.

But there were a few boats out. I could see a speedboat up ahead, towing a skier. There were a couple of fishing vessels out, and a small yacht.

"You think I could get invited to the Peabody's Fourth of July party?" Darcy asked, looking over at the river stone and gray-sided, four-story house to our left.

"Why would you want to go to that?" We all usually

steered clear of the vacationers. It wasn't that they were rude —well, some of them were—but more that they never stuck around, so getting to know them and maintaining friendships was difficult.

"They usually have good food. Plus, I was hoping to bend Mrs. Peabody's ear and see what it would take to get her to consider me for her gallery."

"Ah." I nodded. There it was. Darcy wanted to promote her art. "Why don't you just take a trip to Seattle and talk to her? She might be more receptive to you if you approach her at work and not while she's here on vacation with her family."

I glanced over to see Darcy chewing on the corner of her mouth, still staring at the house. "Yeah. Maybe." She looked at me. "Would you go with me?"

"To Seattle?"

She nodded. "You know I hate big cities."

A slight frown creased my forehead, and I let my kayak glide again. I didn't much care for them, either. "I don't know, Darce. I've got a lot going on."

"Please? It would just be for a couple of days. Overnight. You have the best head for business of the three of us. I'd take Mom, but—"

I waved a hand. "You don't need to say more." Mom was a brilliant businesswoman, but when it came to her kids, she tended to become a steamroller and any sense of tact went out the window. It was great when someone bullied us growing up; she'd be at the parents' front door, demanding to know what would be done about it. But as adults, we needed to fight our own battles and just have her in our corner when we were down to give us hugs and fill us full of the goodies Dad made.

"So, will you go?"

"I'll think about it."

Darcy's eyes lit up. "Maybe we can turn it into a long

weekend and take Daphne with us. We could do some wedding stuff there. Like go dress shopping. We might be able to get ours at Sheilah's, but I doubt she'll find what she wants there."

That was true. Sheilah's was an eveningwear store, but it dealt mostly with prom styles and wedding parties, not the bride. And so far, Scarlett was striking out on a style Daphne liked. "We'll see. Mom will probably want to go wedding dress shopping, so I don't know if that will work. Plus, I have to look at my schedule and see where I can take off." Scarlett would probably be willing to take over running the truck for a day or two, so long as I had all the baked goods prepped for her.

Darcy's lower lip popped out in a quick pout, but then her expression brightened. "I'm not sure Mom can get away to do that, so we might not have to worry about it. Wedding season is threatening to eat her alive. Her latest brides are, like, the queens of the bridezillas."

I chuckled. "We have to make sure Daphne doesn't turn into one of those. But I will look at my schedule and we'll talk to Mom."

"Great! I know it's not a yes, but I'll take it." Darcy grinned.

"Good, because it's all you're getting." Smiling, I settled back into a steadier rhythm.

A shout from one of the fishing vessels drew our attention. We looked over to see a man standing on the deck, raising a fish out of the water.

Darcy let out a sharp whistle. The man looked up with a wide smile and gave us a thumbs up.

"Fishing must be slow today. He seemed extra excited," I said.

"Or maybe he's just a jolly fellow."

Chuckling, I shook my head. "Maybe."

We kept going, rounding another bend in the fork, which

brought the small yacht into full view. The sleek, three-story gray and black boat practically disappeared against the dark water and the pine forest behind it. Even the gold trim helped disguise it. The only part of the boat that really stood out was the name, painted in white on the hull. *Night Dragon*.

Mentally, I shook my head. It wasn't the weirdest boat name I'd seen, but it was definitely strange. I didn't know where people came up with these names.

Another shout echoed over the water, but it wasn't from the fisherman we'd left behind. It was a woman, and it came from the fancy yacht up ahead.

I glanced at Darcy, frowning.

"That didn't sound good," she said.

No, it didn't.

I paddled harder and said a prayer no one had fallen overboard. I didn't see anyone in the water, but the starboard side faced us, shielding the water on the port side from view.

As we neared, a blonde woman in a gauzy pink dress burst from the cabin and onto the aft deck. She stumbled toward the railing on the far side. Slamming into the hull, she grabbed at the rail and missed. For a moment, she disappeared from view. A few seconds later, she popped up again, but couldn't hold her footing and stumbled backward.

"What is wrong with her?" Darcy asked. "You think she's drunk?"

Frowning, I kept my eyes on her. "I don't know. Maybe. But she's going to fall over if she's not careful. There's no rail on the swim platform."

A few seconds later, she did exactly what I feared. As the boat started up, the propellers created enough churn to rock the vessel. The woman, already unsteady on her feet, took several clumsy steps backward and tumbled off the deck into the water. Blonde hair and the pink fabric of her sundress billowed out around her.

"Crap!"

Darcy's exclamation matched what ricocheted through my mind. Without discussion, we dipped our oars into the water, racing toward the yacht.

To my horror, the engines revved. A moment later, it moved, pulling away from the woman.

"Hey!" I waved my arms and paddle, attempting to get the captain's attention.

But the boat didn't slow. Instead, it picked up speed and drove away, headed for the main body of the lake.

Growling in frustration, I dipped my oar back into the water.

As we paddled, we watched the fabric disappear beneath the surface. My heart thumped from exertion and from fear of what we'd find once we reached the spot where she went underwater.

It took us several minutes to reach the area. Once we did, nary a ripple disturbed the water to suggest where the woman vanished beneath the lake's glassy surface.

"Is this the spot?" Darcy held her oar straight, using it to slow her forward movement.

I did the same. "I think so." I'd locked my eyes on the woman's location as we paddled, not even taking them off for a moment to check that Darcy was with me. I didn't want to lose the place where she went down. We'd never find her if we didn't go in right where she sank.

Setting my paddle down across the bow of my kayak, I took off my life jacket.

"What are you doing." Darcy stared at me with alarm in her brown eyes.

"Going in." If she'd been able to, the woman would have surfaced by now.

"What? No, you can't. You know there are all sorts of obstacles down there."

She was right—the lake was full of tree trunks and boulders from when the dam was first constructed and flooded the valley—but I couldn't let that stop me.

I held out a hand and gestured to the water. "Do you see her? If she has any chance, one of us has to go down there, and I'm a better swimmer."

Muscles worked in Darcy's jaw. "Fine. But take a lead." She set her paddle down with a clatter beside her legs and reached for her safety kit. A couple of seconds later, she had a bundle of paracord in her hand.

I slid off my kayak and swam the few feet to her, holding out a hand.

She passed me the end. "Tie it to your shorts."

Quickly, I threaded it through a belt loop. It wouldn't hold if pulled too hard, but it would work as a guide back to the surface.

"Are you sure about this?" Concern pinched Darcy's features.

"No. But we don't have a choice. See if you can get a signal on your phone while I'm under and call for help." I took a deep breath and let it out, then another, stretching my lungs.

Darcy nodded. "Be careful."

Holding her gaze, I inhaled another breath, then dove under.

Thirteen

Almost immediately darkness closed around me like a wet, dirty wool blanket. Thanks to some recent rain, the water clarity was quite poor. I knew what I was doing was a bit of a Hail Mary, but I had to try.

Diving down, I kept my eyes open, hoping for a glimmer of something. A flash of silky hair or a wisp of that pretty pink dress. Anything to guide me.

After a minute of searching and nothing, I popped to the surface, gulping in a breath. Swiping water from my eyes, I spun, searching for my sister. She was a few feet away, corralling my kayak and staring at the water.

"Darce, give me a flashlight."

Darcy turned in her seat at the sound of my voice, then immediately spun back and reached between her feet. A moment later, she raised a waterproof plastic flashlight and tossed it gently to me.

I caught it, inhaled a breath and went under again. A few feet down, I flipped on the light, using it to guide me down.

Deeper and deeper I went, knowing a body without a lungful of air would sink faster than my own.

I reached what I figured to be fifteen or twenty feet and stopped. Slowly, I rotated, my eyes straining in the murk.

A shadow a few feet away caught my attention. Lungs burning, I kicked, heading for it.

Light bounced off something pale in the water ten feet below me and to my right.

I kicked harder.

Ghostly white flesh and a slender arm appeared.

My heart skipped.

Thrusting my hand through the flashlight wristlet, I reached out and snagged the woman's arm, halting her descent. There was no resistance in her muscles. She was a dead weight.

I secured my grip and gave a powerful kick toward the surface.

Fire burned through my chest and made my arms quiver. I'd been down too long.

Stars danced in front of me and the edges of my vision grayed. Where was the surface? I had to be close.

A tug on the back of my pants gave me a quick burst of energy. Darcy wouldn't let me drown.

Putting everything I had into my legs, I kicked, praying I saw light soon.

The gray closing in turned black and narrowed my sight to just pinpoints. An ache formed in my chest as dismay took hold.

I wasn't going to make it.

The tug on my shorts grew, taking on more of my weight and propelling me upward. My feet slowed.

Suddenly, light exploded in my head. I winced and gasped. As I realized what I'd done, I also realized I hadn't inhaled a mouthful of lake water.

It was air that filled my lungs!

"Delaney!"

I gulped in another greedy breath and the blackness

receded. A few stars remained, but some of the starch returned to my muscles. I pulled on the woman's arm, bringing her to the surface.

"Holy cow, you found her!"

I heard the splash of Darcy's paddle in the water as she moved closer.

"Here." She pulled up beside me. "Let's get her into your kayak." Reaching down, she helped me hold on to her.

"Did you… call for help?" I readjusted my grip on the woman, heaving her higher out of the water.

"Yes. I don't know how long it'll take to reach us, though."

Probably a while. We were a ways from town, and it was hard to tell where the Fish and Game boat was. It could be on the other side of the lake and up another fork.

I turned the woman and wrapped an arm around her waist, trying to get her high enough to put her on my kayak. But she was too heavy and too much of a dead weight.

"Darcy, I can't lift her." I grabbed the edge of the boat and leaned my head against the side. I could breathe now, but the dive had taken a lot out of me.

"Wrap the paracord under her arms. I'll try to pull her up."

That was a good idea. Mustering some strength from my reserve tank, I did what she suggested. It took several tries, and we had to lash our kayaks together with my oar through the webbing, but we finally created a stable enough base to pull her out of the water.

Once she was out, Darcy held my kayak steady so I could climb on with her. When we were both on it, I rolled her over to check her pulse. I already knew she wasn't breathing, but I was hoping the colder water down low had given her an edge on the survival game.

Darcy's gasp echoed my own.

My hand froze near her neck as I stared down at the red

stain around a hole in the bodice of her dress just below her sternum.

"Is that—" Darcy pointed, her hand trembling violently.

"It sure looks like it." Swallowing hard, I forced my muscles to move and checked her pulse.

Stillness met my finger, of which I was not surprised. She was practically the color of fresh snow.

"She's dead, isn't she?"

I looked up at my sister and nodded. "Yeah. I think so." I glanced at the woman again, this time taking in her facial features.

Another gasp escaped me. It couldn't be.

"What? Did she move?" Darcy leaned closer.

"No. Look who it is."

Darcy frowned. "Should I know her? I don't."

"It's Felicity Brunswick."

Eyes going wide, Darcy blinked. "You're sure?"

"Yes, I'm sure."

"Do we try CPR?"

Grimacing—not because I didn't want to, but because I doubted it would do any good—I nodded. "Can you tow us in while I try?" It would have to be me who worked on her. For Darcy to do it, we'd have to shuffle Felicity around, losing even more precious seconds.

"Yes."

While Darcy went to work re-rigging the boats together, I adjusted Felicity to a better angle. This would not be easy no matter how I tried it. Knowing I couldn't use both hands without the motion tipping us over, I leaned forward and wound a hand in the webbing that ran along the sides and connected the mesh pockets on both ends. With the other hand, I began chest compressions. Every thirty beats, I puffed two breaths into her lungs. I doubted much air was reaching the structures that it needed to, though. Her lungs were probably full of water.

And even then, I doubted she had the blood volume to carry oxygen around her body. She was so pale.

But still I tried. All the way to shore, I pumped and breathed. When the water became shallow enough to touch, I hopped off and dragged Felicity into the water and up onto the bank. There, Darcy took over, letting me rest.

I sank onto the moss-covered ground, leaves rustling under my palms, sticking to them. Raising my knees, I bent forward to rest my head on them. My chest heaved as I sucked air into my lungs.

For several minutes I sat there, numb to everything, and focused on letting my body recover. I could hear Darcy counting quietly under her breath. Birds chirped overhead, their cheerfulness out of place for the dire scene taking place only feet away.

The sound of an engine entered the mix. The high-pitched whine of the open throttle quickly grew louder. I lifted my head and saw the excited fisherman we'd passed earlier approaching. Dispatch must have put out a radio transmission to all boats on the lake.

I climbed to my feet, my legs quivering. I locked my knees, steadying myself, then walked toward the waterline as he cut the throttle and coasted in.

"What happened? You two all right?" The man's gaze went from me to Darcy, who still knelt above Felicity performing CPR.

"We're okay. Is help coming? She's…" I trailed off and glanced back, swallowing hard, unable to believe the words about to exit my mouth. Things like this just didn't happen here. "She's been shot," I said.

The fisherman's eyes grew round, the whites showing, and the color leached from his face. "What? You're sure?"

I nodded. Disbelief, horror, anger, and sadness all warred in my belly. I couldn't stand still and talk right now. Turning, I hurried over to Darcy, needing to help.

"You breathe," I said, kneeling on Felicity's other side.

Darcy looked up through her lashes, continuing compressions. "You good now?"

"Yes. Switch me." I held up my hands, clasped back to front.

She leaned back and lifted her hands. Mine took their place.

The fisherman walked up to us, hovering a few feet away. "How can… can I help?"

"What's your name?" Darcy asked.

"Ray."

"Do you have a defibrillator on board your boat, Ray?"

"I do, actually." With a crunch of leaves and sticks, he spun around and hurried back to the water.

I kept pumping on Felicity's chest, pausing every fifteen beats now for Darcy to puff in two breaths. Distantly, I heard some splashing and then the dull thump and the wet squeak of rubber on metal as Ray climbed back aboard his boat.

A minute later, he returned and dropped into the dirt beside Darcy.

"Do you know how to work that thing?" Darcy nodded to the small rectangular pack he set on the ground.

"Yes."

He walked her through placing the sensors while I kept up compressions. Once they had everything placed, he asked me to stop, then activated the machine.

I watched the small screen as a flat green line crawled across it. My heart sank. I'd watched enough ambulance shows and medical dramas to know we couldn't shock that.

The machine advised us to continue CPR, so I went back to chest compressions.

For the next fifteen minutes, we traded out. When the Fish and Game officers finally arrived with a paramedic crew in tow, we still hadn't recovered a pulse.

Now past exhausted, I fell back, finding a patch of moss to park my butt on, and sat while the medical crew took over.

Darcy folded herself into a sitting position next to me. She nudged my shoulder. "You all right?"

"Not sure," I answered truthfully. I was too numb to feel much of anything. My brain had shut off somewhere in the water and had yet to truly turn back on. First, it was from nearly passing out and drowning, then it was the shock of seeing who I'd pulled from the depths. There was also the fact that I'd performed CPR twice in just a few days. And on members of the same family. It was all just too much.

Darcy shifted closer, pressing her arm to mine, offering silent comfort.

Pressure swelled behind my eyes and in my nose as tears threatened. While that was better than feeling numb, I didn't want to break down. Not yet and certainly not here.

Sucking a deep breath in through my nose, I forced my mind to focus on the world around me and out of my memories. There would be plenty of time to remember the eerie, all-encompassing darkness of the lake and the feel of Felicity's lifeless body in my arms later.

A shudder went through me.

Darcy glanced over. "You're cold. I should have thought of that. You're soaked." She got up. "Hang on."

Before I could tell her I was fine and not terribly cold, that it was more a reaction to the mental and emotional trauma, she was up and approaching one of the Fish and Game officers. When she returned, she had a three-by-four-inch silver packet in her hands.

Dropping to her knees, she unfolded it, shaking it out with a loud crinkle. It was one of those foil blankets. Whipping it out behind me, she settled it over my shoulders. Immediately, a bit of the chill receded as the thin blanket blocked the air from reaching my skin.

"I hope that helps. It's the best we can do for now."

"It's fine," I muttered. It would take the edge off, but to truly dry out and warm up to normal, I needed a hot shower and dry clothes.

I resisted the urge to scoff. *That* wasn't happening anytime soon.

As we sat there, the paramedics stopped CPR and covered Felicity's body with a blanket. They'd come to the same conclusion we had, even though we'd kept trying. No amount of resuscitation would bring her back.

Felicity Brunswick was dead.

Fourteen

Over the next ten minutes, more boats arrived, which meant more people. Soon, the small bank where we'd come ashore was full of medical and law enforcement personnel.

Including Detective Fiore.

Rolling my shoulders, I tucked my head and did my best to become invisible. I could only imagine what Jack would think when he found out I was involved.

Probably that I had something to do with it. With both deaths.

Which was ludicrous. But I couldn't fault the logic of someone thinking I killed them both. I was the only witness to Phil's death. Now, today, my alibi for Felicity's was my sister.

It didn't look good.

I raised my eyes, looking toward shore through my lashes.

Like a tractor beam, Jack turned and met my gaze.

Quickly, I looked down.

Twigs and leaves crunched under heavy-soled shoes. A shadow fell over me, and a pair of worn brown leather hiking boots entered my field of vision.

For several seconds, he stood there and said nothing.

I chanced a glance up through my lashes at his face.

Thunderclouds decorated his expression, turning his already dark eyes the color of midnight. A muscle ticked in his jaw.

"Why are you here? At a crime scene. Again."

I lifted a shoulder and looked at Darcy. She held up her hands in the universal, "Don't look at me," gesture.

With a sigh, I turned back to Jack. "Apparently, I'm a murder magnet."

He snorted. "Yep. What happened? I got a very quick overview from dispatch. I don't even know who the victim is yet. I stepped off the boat intending to find that out first, then I saw you sitting here." He thrust a hand toward me.

"Felicity Brunswick," I muttered.

He stilled, an intense frown drawing his brows together. "What did you say?"

I pulled in a breath through my nose, then let it out with a quick huff. My gaze met his. "The victim. It's Felicity Brunswick."

Jack shifted, turning to look at the blanket-covered body. He swiped a hand down his face and then through his hair, gripping the strands. Under his breath, he muttered a soft curse.

"Okay." He dropped his hand. "Start at the beginning and tell me what happened." He took a small notebook and a pen from the pocket of his black tactical pants.

Darcy and I exchanged a quick look. I could tell by the set to her face, she didn't want to do the talking.

"We were at lunch at the inn," I said. "Daphne and Morgan want to get married in October, so there's a lot to do. When Mom went into planning mode, asking about a bunch of things that didn't require our input"—I waved a finger between myself and Darcy—"we decided to take the kayaks out. It was completely random that we came up the western fork."

"We wanted to look at the houses," Darcy said, nodding across the water at the mansion perched in the trees.

Jack glanced back briefly. "All right. Continue. What did you see?"

"Not much, honestly." I chewed on my lip, trying to remember if there was anyone else on the boat before Felicity appeared. "We came up the channel, passed a fisherman, then rounded the bend and the yacht Felicity was on came fully into view."

"You could see it before you rounded the bend?" Jack asked.

I nodded. "Just the bow. It was close to shore on this side."

"Okay, go on."

I ran my tongue over my bottom lip and stared out at the water. "As we got closer, we heard a woman shout. A few moments later, Felicity stumbled out of the cabin. Though we didn't know it was her then."

"And we do mean stumbled," Darcy added. "She looked like she was drunk. Slammed into the railing, fell down, then tumbled right off the swim deck when the boat moved."

"Did you see anyone? Hear a gunshot?"

"No," I said. "The boat just revved its engines and sailed off. We tried to flag it down, but it kept going."

"What was the name of the boat?"

"*Night Dragon*," Darcy answered.

Jack raised an eyebrow, but jotted the name down. "Okay. What happened then? You went after her? Dispatch said bystanders pulled the woman from the water. That was you?"

"Yes." I pulled the foil blanket tighter around my shoulders. The rustling sound it made grated on my nerves and sent a shiver down my spine. "She sort of floated at the surface for a minute or so before she disappeared. I kept my eyes locked on the spot, and we didn't stop until we were right over it. Darcy called for help while I dove down hoping to locate her." The press of tears made my face ache. My jaw worked as I glanced away, trying to fight them back. I still wasn't ready to cry.

"It's a miracle you did. The water isn't the clearest even on a good day, and we've had too much rain to call it that."

I hunched my shoulders and looked past him. "Yeah." I honestly didn't know how I found her. Luck and divine intervention, I suppose.

"So, was she alive when you brought her up? Or couldn't you tell?"

"We didn't check until we had her on the kayak. At that point, she didn't have a pulse. I don't know about before that. But I did CPR while Darcy towed us to shore."

Both of his dark brows winged upward. "You did CPR on a moving kayak?"

I nodded once.

"How?"

"It wasn't easy. Balance and adrenaline, I guess."

Admiration flared to life in the depths of his eyes, and his expression softened slightly. He shook his head, some disbelief showing on his face. "Okay, then what happened?"

"We got her to shore and continued CPR. The fisherman found us. He had an AED onboard, but it was too late. She didn't have a shockable rhythm. We kept trying until the paramedics arrived, but—" I broke off, gesturing to the blanket draped mound on the forest floor.

Jack turned to look as well, staying silent for several long beats. He tapped his notepad against his hand. "Do you know who owns the *Night Dragon?*

I glanced at Darcy as I slowly shook my head. She did too.

"No," I said, turning back to him. "But that shouldn't be hard to figure out. It would be registered."

"You could ask Ray—the fisherman." Darcy pointed. "He

might know. He also might have seen which way it went. It would have passed him as he came toward us."

"All right." Jack backed up a step. "You two sit tight. I might have more questions later." Spinning on his booted foot, he headed for the nearest deputy.

I blew out a breath and leaned my elbows on my knees, closing my eyes.

Darcy nudged me. "So…"

Turning my head, but leaving it propped on my hands, I looked at her. "So?"

"So, we're definitely going with Jack as your romantic prospect, if only so he can keep you out of trouble."

I groaned. "Not even funny, Darcy."

She chuckled. "It's kinda funny."

I let out a long-suffering sigh.

"Hey," she tapped my arm. "It's either laugh or cry right now."

Lifting my head, I took a better look at her face. Behind the smile, I could see the battle against the tears. I raised an arm, inviting her into my space blanket cocoon. "Come here."

She grimaced, looking me up and down. "You're soaked."

I rolled my eyes and hooked an arm around her shoulders, anyway. "You'll dry."

For over an hour, the two of us sat there like that and watched the beehive of activity. Jack interviewed Ray, then talked to the paramedics and the crime scene unit. Eventually, he circled around to us.

"Do you two want a ride back to the inn? I'm guessing you don't want to paddle back?"

We both shook our heads.

"Heck, no," Darcy said.

He motioned for us to stand. "Come on. We'll drop you off."

I stood up, still huddling under the Mylar blanket. "You're leaving the scene already?"

"Fish and Game tracked down the yacht. Your family's inn is on the way."

My eyes widened. "You have her killer in custody?"

He pressed his lips together, scowling. "No. Unfortunately the boat was empty when they came across it." He waved us forward. "Come on."

I frowned, disappointed. Of course it was empty. That would have been too easy.

We followed him to the shore, where a deputy passed our kayaks to his colleague on the boat. Darcy hopped on without assistance, but my legs were wobbly, probably from all the exertion. Not to mention the adrenaline dump.

Holding the crinkly Mylar around my neck with one hand, I gingerly stepped onto the stern. It rocked and I rocked with it, losing my balance.

Strong hands gripped my arm and around my waist, keeping me from falling in the water.

"I've got you."

Jack's low voice rumbled in my ear.

Oh my…

A different sort of off-kilter feeling rolled through me.

Clearing my throat, I eased away from his torso. I should not be having such feelings right now. Not when my over-whelming desire was to cry and then sleep.

Maybe that's why I was having these feelings. It was a trauma response.

Yes. I liked that theory. It certainly wasn't because Darcy was right and there was something there between me and the detective. I barely knew him, so those kinds of feelings were ridiculous.

"Thank you," I mumbled.

"Of course."

He let go of my waist, but kept hold of my arm, helping me board the boat. Once I was on, I moved to sit next to

Darcy along the railing to the right of the open bridge, and he and a second deputy jumped on behind me.

"Are we ready?" the deputy at the helm asked.

Jack gave him a thumbs up.

The engines rumbled to life. I settled into my seat and tucked the crinkly blanket tighter around myself, warding off the breeze that would hit as soon as we sped up. Even though it was warm outside, and I'd mostly dried off, there was still a bone-deep chill in my body.

The trip back down the fork and into the main body of the lake was much quicker than our paddle had been. Within ten minutes, we were nearing the shore at the inn.

Part of me expected to see our family gathered on the dock, waiting, but I knew we hadn't been gone long enough for anyone to even get mildly worried.

Throttling back, the patrol boat pulled up to the dock. Jack and the second deputy jumped off, grabbing lines and pulling the boat closer to the pilings.

Still unsteady on my legs, I stood. Through sheer will, I kept myself from swaying and followed Darcy to the stern. She took Jack's hand and hopped off.

Then it was my turn. He held out both arms, grasping my free hand with one and placing the other on my side to guide me onto the dock.

"You good?"

I looked up into the dark depths of his eyes and nodded. "Thank you."

"You're welcome."

Offering him a tight smile, I took a step to move around him, ready to go sit in the shower until the hot water ran out.

"Delaney."

I paused, glancing over.

"I just—" He stopped, pressing his lips into a thin line and glancing out over the water for a moment. "What you did—" He stopped again and shook his head, looking down, before sucking in a breath and meeting my gaze. "You did good today."

My lips parted ever so slightly in surprise. I hadn't expected that. "Oh. Um, thank you."

He nodded once and stepped toward the boat. "Go get warmed up."

I shrugged my space blanket higher up on my neck.

"If you remember anything else, call me." He hopped onboard.

"I will. Stay safe." I backed up as the second deputy jumped on, having unloaded our kayaks.

Jack nodded.

As the engines revved, I took a few steps up the dock, watching until Jack turned around and the boat pulled away.

A pleasant warmth unfurled in my chest, chasing away some of the emotional chill. If this was a trauma response, it was unlike any other.

I scoffed at myself and rolled my eyes. I'd never experienced trauma like this before, so I didn't really have anything to compare it to.

Get your head in the game, Delaney.

There were no *feelings* there for Detective Fiore. My brain was in survival mode and needed a reset. It was grasping at anything and everything as it tried to make sense of the last few hours.

"Laney, you coming?"

I turned at the sound of Darcy's voice. "Yeah." Feet thumping on the wooden dock, I followed her onto shore.

Fifteen

With a huff, I rolled over—again—and pulled the comforter higher on my face, tucking the edge under my chin. I should be sound asleep. Heaven knew I was tired. My limbs ached from yesterday's exertion, but it didn't seem to matter. My brain simply wouldn't shut off.

Who killed Felicity Brunswick?

Why?

Did it have something to do with her husband or was it completely unrelated?

My bet was on the former.

But what did they do?

Before her death, I would have put money on Felicity being behind her husband's murder. Maybe not the one who actually did it; my guess would have been she hired someone. But after talking to her and learning she lied about why she came to see him at work the day he died, she made the most sense.

Now, though, I had no clue. The son? Maybe he wanted to inherit all of his father's estate. Or maybe Felicity tried to challenge the will.

It could have been a disgruntled client too. But then, that

didn't explain why Felicity was killed. Unless she knew something the client didn't want getting out. She did have access to her husband's work files.

I sighed and rolled over again, flipping my pillow.

Was that client the one who owned the *Night Dragon*? Mom and Dad didn't know who owned it. Darcy and I asked after we relayed what happened and assured them—multiple times—that we were fine.

And if the client didn't own the boat, who did?

Flopping onto my back, I stared at the ceiling, watching the fan whir softly overhead.

This was ridiculous.

I turned my head and glanced at the clock.

Three-oh-three a.m.

Even if I went to sleep right this second, I wouldn't even get another hour before my alarm went off.

"Screw this." Flinging the covers back, I sat up, swinging my legs over the side.

Millie lifted her head. I couldn't see her eyes in the dark, but she was probably glaring daggers at me.

"Sorry, sweetie. Go back to sleep." Getting up, I gathered some clothes and went into the bathroom to dress.

I slapped at the wall, looking for the light switch, and turned it on, squinting against the sudden brightness.

I'd showered before bed, so I went through an abbreviated routine and left the bathroom.

Millie chirped, hopping onto the counter as I started the coffeemaker. I scratched her ears and stared blankly out the kitchen window as the coffee brewed. I needed to remember to toss a few extra pods in my bag to take with me. I'd need the added jolt today.

After downing a cup and some breakfast, I made another cup to go, fed my cat, then headed out the door. It probably wasn't a bad thing that I was early. I could get a little extra done before Yves dropped off my truck. I could make him a batch of his favorite muffins too.

Stillness engulfed me as I stepped outside. The air had a heaviness to it that sat on my shoulders like a wet blanket. A dog barked down the street, the sound muffled by the thick atmosphere.

A shiver went up my spine. Why was it creepier outside now than when I normally left? It wasn't that much earlier.

Readjusting my grip on my tote, I walked down the steps, eyes moving from one side of the yard to the other. I don't know what I expected to see.

Hopefully nothing.

Something rustled in the bushes by the road. My heart thumped, and I froze, staring into the darkness for several seconds before it clicked in my brain that whatever it was couldn't be a person. The bushes weren't big enough to hide someone.

Shaking my head, I started back down the sidewalk to my car. A gray tiger cat darted out from the bush and across the street.

See? I told myself. Nothing to be worried about. It was just my sleep-deprived brain letting my imagination run wild. Nothing sinister would jump out at me from behind the neighbor's house. Fernwood was a safe place.

Yes, and that's why two people have been murdered.

I scowled and told my subconscious mind to shut up. But I still quickened my pace.

The car beeped as I unlocked it. Getting in, I tossed my tote onto the passenger seat, then relocked the doors. No use borrowing trouble by making it easy for someone to get in.

With a quick touch on the start button, the vehicle roared to life. I waited a moment for the engine to settle, then put it in gear and pointed it toward the church, feeling better once I was on the move. By the time I reached the parking lot and let myself inside, my equilibrium, while not normal, was closer to that than it had been.

Still, as I started down the stairs, I paused, turning around to heed Daphne's warning from the other day and lock the door behind me. For added comfort, I turned the radio on as well before I started baking. I couldn't handle the silence this morning.

Hours later and singing softly to the music on the radio, I wound the ends of a piece of flavorless dental wax around my fingers and slid it under the last cinnamon roll log, slicing off the first roll. Once these went in the oven, I could start frosting cupcakes and sugar cookies.

I'd gotten a lot done this morning. I likely had time to start on the decorations for the next wedding cake on my calendar.

The doors at the top of the stairs rattled, making me jump.

"Hello?" Yves's muffled voice floated down from above.

"Coming!" I called. Quickly slicing the last two rolls, I set them on the baking sheet and wiped my hands, hurrying around the counter and up the stairs to let him in.

Sunlight streamed inside, making me squint.

"Good morning." Yves smiled at me from the stoop.

I smiled back and stepped aside to let him in. "Hi."

He walked in, and I closed the door.

"Oh, it smells wonderful in here." Sticking his nose in the air, he sniffed.

"Thank you. I baked you some of the raspberry white chocolate muffins you like." Leading him down the steps, I stopped in front of the counter and picked up a bakery box. "Here you go."

"You didn't have to do that." He took the box. "Thank you."

"You're welcome. Thank you for bringing the truck to me. And so early. I really appreciate you working on it outside your normal hours."

He lifted a shoulder. "Not a problem. I was close to done

Friday evening. Just needed to tighten a few things and run some tests to be sure it wasn't leaking. I'm sorry I couldn't get it back to you then, but I had a previous commitment."

I waved a hand. "You're fine. It all worked out. I found a workaround."

"Good. Well"—he reached into his pocket and produced a set of keys—"it's running perfectly now. Do you want to write me a check? Or I can pull up the invoice online and you can pay with a card."

"I brought my checkbook, hang on." Turning, I walked into the kitchen and dug into my tote. He told me the amount, and I wrote it out. It wasn't as bad as I feared.

Ripping the paper from the booklet, I handed it to him. "Thank you, again, Yves."

"Anytime, Delaney." He accepted the check and put it in his pocket. "Thank you for the muffins."

A bright smile wreathed my face. "You're welcome. Let me just stow these rolls and I can take you back to your shop." Rounding the counter again, I lifted the roll pans and slid them into my tabletop proofer. Luckily, I had everything out of the oven for now, so I wouldn't have to worry about that.

Grabbing my keys and my wallet, I left the kitchen and motioned for Yves to precede me up the stairs.

As I followed him a thought occurred to me. "Yves?"

He glanced back.

"Can I ask you something?"

"Sure." He paused at the door.

"I know you don't work on boat engines, but do you happen to know who owns the *Night Dragon*?"

He mumbled the name under his breath a couple of times, thinking. "Maybe," he finally said. "What does it look like?"

"It's a small yacht. Gray with black accents and gold trim."

He tipped his head. "That sounds like Coral Peabody's boat."

Coral Peabody?

My eyebrows rose. That was a real name? I knew of the Peabodys. Darcy and I passed their house yesterday. But I didn't know any of them were named Coral. She had to be related, though. The name was just too coincidental. "Who is that?" I asked. "Is she one of the vacationers?"

"She is."

"Is she nice? Does she have someone to whom she might lend the vessel?"

"She's nice enough, I suppose." His cheeks colored. "Why are you asking about her?"

I narrowed my eyes. "How well do you know her?"

The redness on his face grew.

Surprise and shock made my eyes go wide. "You—" I paused, lowering my voice. "You've been intimate with her, haven't you?"

A muscle in his jaw ticked. "And? It's not a crime for a man to have a social life."

"I didn't say it was. Have you spoken to her lately?"

He frowned. "No," he answered a little too quickly. "She's in Seattle. Won't be here until the end of the month for the holiday. Why?"

I brought a hand up, pressing it to my lips as I glanced away in thought. Nibbling on a nail, I looked at him. "Who would have access to her boat?"

Turning on the landing, he propped his fists on his hips and the color to his cheeks receded as a hardness entered his eyes. "Why all the questions about the boat?"

I continued to chew on my nail, not wanting to upset him further. "You didn't hear about what happened yesterday?"

He frowned. "No. I—" His mouth flattened, and I could see the debate in his eyes. After several moments, he continued. "Fine. Yes, I've spoken to her recently. I was in Seattle this weekend visiting her. I got home late and went to bed. What happened?"

"Phil Brunswick's wife, Felicity was murdered. On the *Night Dragon*."

Yves' silvery blue eyes went round with shock and his mouth fell open. "What? You're sure?"

"Yes. I watched it happen. Well," I held up a hand. "Not the actual murder. My sister Darcy and I watched her stumble out of the cabin and fall into the water, then the boat drove off. When we pulled her out, she had a gunshot wound to the chest."

He ran a hand over his jaw and mouth, looking away, his eyes still wide.

I crossed my arms. "You should go talk to Detective Fiore. Though I'm sure he probably knows who the registered owner is by now. But it would help your friend for him to know she has an alibi."

"What?" His gaze met mine. He blinked and the thoughtful expression on his face cleared but was replaced by one that looked deeply concerned. "Oh. Yes. Right. Of course." His head bobbed, and he reached behind himself for the doorknob. "I'll—I'll do that." He opened the door. "Thanks for the muffins. See you later, Delaney."

Confusion furrowed my forehead as I walked out after him. "Where are you going? Don't you need a ride?"

He stopped, glancing around the parking lot. "Right. I guess I do."

I pointed to my SUV, then pushed the button on my fob to unlock the doors. He got in, and I went around to the driver's side and climbed in beside him.

"I'm sorry if I upset you," I said, backing out of the parking space.

"It's fine." He stared out the window. "I just—" He stopped and shook his head. "Never mind."

I opened my mouth, intending to ask again, then thought

better of it. He was basically my captive until we reached his shop, and I didn't want to make him more uncomfortable than he was.

So, I kept my mouth shut and drove, all the while wondering what had made him so… squirrelly.

When we reached his garage, he hopped out before I even put the car in park. With a wave and a quick, "Thanks," he was gone.

"What the heck was that all about?" I muttered, staring after him for several seconds before pulling away. What did he know? Or at least suspect? It could be nothing.

Or it could be he knew who took the boat. Yves could be the key to cracking Felicity's murder. And possibly Phil's if the two were connected.

I sat at the stop sign by the garage and debated what to do. I could go back to the church and continue my work, burying my head in the sand while hoping Yves did what I suggested and talked to Jack. Or I could tell Jack myself.

With a groan, I leaned forward, resting my forehead on the steering wheel. Why did life have to be so difficult sometimes? I didn't want to alienate Yves. He was a nice guy and a great mechanic. I don't know as if I'd call him a friend, but we had an amicable working relationship.

But I wasn't sure I could live with myself if I didn't say anything and a killer got to walk around free.

Sitting up, I put my blinker on, then turned left.

Away from the church.

Sixteen

This was crazy.

Right?

I mean, it could be nothing. I could be completely off-base and complicate Yves's life for no reason.

Chewing on the corner of my bottom lip, I stared at the police station from my parked car. Maybe I should just go back to the church and finish baking. My cinnamon rolls would be ready to go in the oven soon. In fact, they'd be ruined if I didn't take them out of the proofer before long.

But something in my gut said to go inside.

"I better be right about this," I muttered, grabbing the door handle.

Climbing out, I pushed the door shut, then swiped my damp palms on my shorts. Taking a deep breath, I headed inside.

A deputy gave me a bored stare from behind a pane of plexiglass as I entered. I walked up to the speaker set in the window.

"Hi. Um, I need to speak with Detective Fiore. It's about the Brunswick murders."

The man raised an eyebrow. "You a reporter?"

"What?" I frowned, then waved my hands. "No. No, definitely not. I'm a witness. Can you just let him know Delaney Fowler is here? Please?"

He stared at me for another moment, then slowly reached for the phone.

"Hey, it's Charles at the front desk. I've got a Delaney Fowler up here. She wants to talk to you." He paused a moment, listening. His gaze flicked to me, then away again. "All right. I'll send her back."

Relief warred with another surge of anxiety. I swiped my hands on my shorts again.

Deputy Charles set the phone down and walked around his desk to the door. It swung out, and he motioned me in.

We walked down a short hallway that was more of a walkway than anything. Doors lined the wall to the left. To the right, it was open to a sea of desks. He stopped at an office near the end and rapped his knuckles on the open door.

"Come in." Jack's voice carried through the opening.

The deputy stepped back and gestured for me to enter. I thanked him softly and entered the office.

Jack sat behind the desk, wearing his standard uniform of a black department polo. I imagined he had on the black tactical pants and work boots as well but couldn't see below the desk.

"Have a seat, Delaney." Jack motioned to the visitor's chair opposite him. "What can I do for you?"

I perched on the edge of the chair and folded my hands in my lap to keep them still. "I just had a strange conversation with Yves Taskin." I pursed my lips. No. That wasn't quite right. "Well, not strange, exactly. Odd? Weird. I don't know. It—"

Jack waved his hand, halting my babbling. "Just tell me what happened."

"Right." I sucked in a breath through my nose. "So, Yves is my mechanic. He brought my food truck back to me this morning. I've been thinking about that boat that Felicity was on, and since he deals with repairs and such, I thought I'd ask if he knew the owner."

"You asked a car mechanic if he knew who a boat's owner was?"

"I know it sounds strange, but it's the same general field, so yes. I did. Anyway, he did know. And I'm guessing you probably already know who owns it, but he said it's a woman named Coral Peabody."

"You're correct. I already figured that out."

"Well, do you know she lives in Seattle and that's she's there now and was all weekend?"

"I haven't spoken to her, no." His eyes narrowed slightly. "How do you know she's there?" His gaze narrowed further. "Did you call her? Please tell me you didn't."

"Don't worry, I didn't. Yves told me. They're an item. He was there with her all weekend."

A dark brow went up. "Your mechanic is dating an art gallery owner?"

I huffed a quick laugh. "Right? But if you've met Yves, it makes sense. He's very… suave." I waved a hand. "Anyway, that's not really what I came to tell you."

Jack leaned back and crossed muscular arms over his broad chest. "Okay. What is, then?"

"Yves brought me my truck because it was easier for me to give him a ride back to his shop than it was for me to find a ride there—and later home—or for him to come get me, then take me back. I can write a check from anywhere, so…" I shrugged, trailing off. He got the idea, I'm sure.

"As we were wrapping things up, and I mentioned what happened, he got this speculative look on his face when I told him about it. And, honestly, he looked a bit scared too. But he'd already told me he was with her in Seattle, so I don't know why it would bother him that her boat was used.

Unless maybe he knows who had the boat. But, anyway, I told him to come talk to you."

"You don't think he will, do you? That's why you're here, isn't it?"

I wrung my hands together and looked a way for a second. "Yeah," I muttered, turning back to meet his dark gaze. "When we went to leave, he forgot I was taking him back to the shop. I'm not sure he wouldn't have just started walking if I hadn't followed him outside and reminded him. I can't tell you for sure he knows anything, but I think he might at least have an idea about who could have been driving that boat." I paused, rolling my lips in and pressing them together. "I know this is all speculation, but the weirdness vibe I got from our conversation won't let me let it go."

Jack dropped his arms and sat forward again. He drew a notepad closer and picked up a pen. "Yves Taskin, you said?"

I nodded.

"Spell that."

I did, and he wrote it down.

"Okay. I'll look into it. Thank you for the tip." Glancing up, he offered me a polite smile.

"You're welcome." I shifted, moving to get up, having said what I came to say, when another thought struck me. "Did you find out what was in the file Felicity brought to her husband?"

He squinted. "Yes."

I raised an eyebrow. "And?"

"And it's none of your business."

"Oh." I blinked. "Right. Of course. Sorry." Standing, I stepped around the chair. "I'll just... go... now." I pointed at the door.

Jack nodded once. "Thank you for the information."

"You're welcome."

"And Delaney?"

I glanced back as I reached the door. "Hmm?"

"Please stay out of this. Two people are dead, and I don't need you making yourself a target."

My frown returned, deeper than ever. "I'm not actively out seeking information, Jack. I'm just talking to people."

"Exactly. Stop it."

A soft chuckle of disbelief escaped. "You want me to stop talking to people."

He scowled. "You know what I mean. Don't twist my words."

"I'm not."

"Uh-huh. Sure." He let out a sigh. "Just... please stay out of this?"

When the scowl disappeared and concern overtook it, any desire I had to argue with him evaporated. A warmth unfurled in my belly. It was kind of nice that he was worried about me. He shouldn't be, because I could handle myself, but it was still nice. "I'll behave."

After giving me another narrow-eyed look, he nodded once. "Do that. Now, go back to work, please, and let me do my job."

"No problem. My cinnamon rolls are probably deflating as we speak." Offering him a quick wave, I hurried away.

My palms were less sweaty now, but I still hoped I did the right thing coming here.

Seventeen

"Oh, I like that one, Delaney." Daphne stood from her seat on the plush tan couch and came closer as I walked toward the mirror.

I turned slightly, staring at my reflection. "Yeah?" We were at Sheilah's Formalwear, picking out bridesmaid's dresses. I liked this one too. The rich red fabric draped across my torso from one shoulder to the opposite side, where it gathered near my waist and then flowed like water down to the floor.

Darcy emerged from the dressing room next to mine, wearing the same dress. "I like this one too."

"I think it's the one, then." Daphne smiled brightly. "It'll look good on Natasha and Aislyn too." She mimed wiping her forehead. "Phew. That's one thing off the list."

I chuckled. "We'll mark your dress off this weekend." Darcy had taken it upon herself to organize the Seattle trip. Somehow, she'd secured an interview with Ms. Peabody on Saturday. Mom's schedule wouldn't allow her to get away, so we planned to video conference her in on the store's Zoom account so she could be part of the fun. With that detail settled, it was enough to convince Daphne to go. We planned to leave Friday afternoon, spending the evening strolling through the city, then visit Coral Peabody's gallery on Saturday morning before we shopped until we dropped for wedding items.

And I prayed no one told Detective Fiore we stopped in Ms. Peabody's gallery, even if the Brunswicks' deaths weren't the reason we were going there. He already wasn't pleased with my involvement.

"Well, I'm glad this went quickly," Daphne said, returning to the couch. "I should be home about the same time Morgan gets off work."

"He had to work late again?" Darcy asked.

"Yeah. They're trying to pick up the slack from Phil's cases. And Mandi's departure."

I looked at my sister with a shocked frown. "What? She quit?"

"Yeah. Morgan said it was never really a secret in the office she and Phil had a thing, but Felicity didn't know. Well, someone told her. She showed up Friday afternoon and pitched a royal fit. Accused the woman of murdering her husband." Daphne rolled her eyes. "That woman couldn't hurt a flea. And I don't know why Felicity was so up in arms. I'd bet my retirement fund she's been having an affair too."

I blinked, eyes wide. "What? She showed up there Friday?" That was the day I'd seen her at her house.

"Yep. Nile got between them when Felicity lunged at her. He made her leave, but Morgan said Mandi was so upset, she handed Nile her key and told him she quit. Then she just left."

"Whoa. She was at that wedding I catered on Saturday. She *and* her husband."

"Oh, I bet that was interesting," Daphne said.

"Yeah, but not for the reason you think. Some guy there made a pass at her because he heard she was already stepping out on her husband with Phil. Her husband was drunk and attacked the guy. Detective Fiore broke it up."

"Wait." Darcy held up a hand. "Your detective was there? And when did we go back to Detective Fiore instead of Jack?"

I rolled my eyes. "He's not my detective." I chose to ignore her second question.

"Whatever." She waved a hand. "What was he doing there?"

"He was a guest. The groom is a friend." I propped a hand on my hip, my mind spinning with this new information. "I wonder if he knows about the incident between the two women? And that Mandi quit. He didn't mention it when I talked to him on Monday."

Daphne frowned. "When did you talk to him Monday?"

"I had some information to share." I said a silent prayer they wouldn't press the issue. I didn't want to spread gossip about Yves. Especially since I didn't know what Jack had done with the information or what he'd found out about what the man knew.

"About the murders?"

"Yes. Just something I remembered," I lied. "It probably wasn't anything, but any detail could be important."

Darcy gave me a wicked smile. "You just wanted to see Jack." She waggled her eyebrows.

I rolled my eyes, dropping my arm back to my side. "Would you stop? I told you Sunday I wasn't interested in him."

"I still don't believe you."

I shrugged. "You can believe whatever you want." Turning, I headed for the dressing room. "I'm going to change."

Her ornery giggle followed me out of the room.

Shutting myself in the dressing room, I sighed. The idea that sparked during our paddle on Sunday to casually date was holding more and more merit. It would get her off my back.

I huffed. Actually, she'd probably just start asking when

we would get serious and settle down. And Mom would chime in her two cents too.

Grumbling under my breath about annoying sisters, I changed out of the dress, then went back to the showroom.

It took us nearly thirty minutes to check-out; Daphne had to order for her other two bridesmaids who lived in Seattle. With sales receipts in hand and a promise that the dresses would be in with several weeks to spare, we left.

"I wish it wasn't so late," Darcy said. "We could stop and get coffee."

I held up a finger. "It might be too late for coffee, but Strayer's Ice Cream Shoppe is open." During the summer, the store kept long hours. It was only a little after seven, but the shop would be open until ten.

"Ooo." Daphne spun on her heel. "Let's go."

Laughing, I glanced at Darcy. "I guess we're getting ice cream."

"I guess so." She looped her arm through mine. "Come on."

We quickly caught up to Daphne and made our way to the corner, where we needed to cross the street to get to the ice cream shop. Darcy pushed the button to activate the crosswalk signal, then we waited.

"So, did you rearrange your schedule so you can get off work early on Friday?" Darcy asked Daphne.

"I did. Leanna's—"

Daphne didn't get to finish her sentence. A squeal of tires and a revving engine cut her off.

We turned toward the sound.

All the air froze in my lungs and my feet grew roots at the sight of a black SUV barreling toward us.

Eighteen

"**L**ookout!"

The shout from across the street galvanized me into action. Daphne had turned, taking a step back. I grabbed her hand and spun around, running into Darcy like a linebacker. Together, the three of us dove toward the storefront behind us.

Pain radiated through my left elbow and hip as we landed on the doorstep of Eastman's Pharmacy. Tires sped by our feet, missing Darcy by inches.

Hair drifted over my face from the breeze created by the car speeding by. It bumped over the curb, just missing a car stopped at the light.

I raised my hand to push the lock of hair back, then groaned as the pain in my elbow increased.

This was not good.

Grimacing, I sat up, cradling my arm, and looked at my sisters. "Are you guys okay?"

"I think so." Daphne rolled to sit up.

"Yeah. That was too close." Darcy, already sitting, got to her feet. "Thank you for tackling me."

"Not a problem." Wincing, I shifted to stand, but the movement jostled my arm. I let out a cry of pain.

"Delaney?" Daphne got to her knees and shuffled closer. "Are you all right?"

"No. I think—" I glanced at my arm, swallowing hard as another wave of pain radiated up it. "I think maybe I broke my arm."

Dr. Eastman, the pharmacist who owned the drugstore, ran outside. "Oh my goodness. Girls, are you okay?" He crouched in front of us, concern drawing down his eyebrows.

"Darcy and I are all right, but Delaney's hurt." Daphne gestured to my arm.

"Okay. Come on. Let's get you up."

With his help and Darcy's, I was able to get to my feet without making the pain worse. They helped me to a bench nearby while Daphne called the police.

"Who was that?" I glanced over, but the SUV had disappeared.

"I don't know," Darcy said. "I barely saw it."

"There was a woman driving," Daphne said.

My brows knit together. "You're sure?" If any of us had caught a glimpse of the driver, it would have been her. She'd been the closest to the street and had faced that direction the longest.

She nodded. "I saw long blonde hair. I couldn't make out her face, though. She had on big sunglasses."

"What about a license plate?" Dr. Eastman glanced at her while he examined my arm.

"I didn't catch that." Daphne frowned.

"Me, either," Darcy said.

"Well, hopefully, someone else did," Dr. Eastman said. He looked up at me. "Can you move it at all?"

I shook my head. "Not without a lot of pain."

"Where?"

"In my elbow. I landed on it." It throbbed steadily now,

each beat like a shard of glass cutting through the deep layers of skin and muscle.

I blinked back tears. This was bad. So, so bad. How could I bake with only one arm? At least it was my non-dominant arm, so I might be able to still do some things, like decorate. But kneading dough and holding bowls while stirring? Not everything could go in my mixers.

Sirens sounded down the street. Two separate ones. I glanced down the road and saw a police car coming. About a block behind it an ambulance followed. We weren't far from the fire and police stations.

Moments later, the emergency vehicles pulled up, parking along the curb. A bit of relief went through me as I saw the cop who emerged. It was Alex Hauser. We'd grown up together, graduating in the same class.

"Delaney?" Alex strode closer. His gaze moved to my sisters. "Daphne? Darcy? What happened?"

"Someone jumped the curb and nearly hit us." Daphne pointed in the direction in which the car disappeared.

He glanced back. "Which car?"

"They drove off," Darcy said. "It was a black SUV. None of us caught the plate."

"But it was a woman driving," Daphne added.

"Okay. I'll see what else I can find out." He looked over his shoulder at the ambulance that just pulled up. "Will you three be okay until they come over?" He tipped his head toward the medical crew emerging from the ambulance.

"We're fine. Go find that—" Daphne broke off, clamping her lips together as storm clouds gathered in her eyes. "Just go find her."

He nodded once. "I'll do my best." Spinning on his heel, he walked away.

My gaze traveled past him to the paramedics making their way toward us. I hoped they carried the good stuff, because the pain in my arm was only increasing.

"Hello." The older of the two medics smiled as she approached me. "I'm Lindsay. What's your name?"

"Delaney."

"Nice to meet you, Delaney. Can you tell me what happened?" Her gaze flicked to the arm I cradled.

"A car jumped the curb. We dove out of the way, but I landed on my elbow."

The woman winced. "Ouch. Okay, let's take a quick look."

Muscles clenching, I steeled myself for the pain as she crouched in front of me. "It really hurts when I move."

Lindsay nodded. "I'll try not to shift it. I just want to have a bit of a feel."

That didn't sound much better.

With gentle fingers, she probed my elbow. White-hot pokers zinged through my arm when she hit a spot on the underside of my forearm. Hissing, I shifted away.

"Yeah, it's a bit crunchy feeling. Okay, let's get that stabilized." She turned to her partner. "Let's get IV access and get some morphine onboard, then we'll splint it."

My shoulders sagged with relief. Morphine sounded wonderful.

While they worked to make me comfortable, another police unit arrived as well as an unmarked car. Just as the morphine hit, I saw a shock of dark hair and a muscular physique emerge from the dark blue sedan.

Jack.

The world tilted. *Whoa.* My head suddenly weighed a hundred pounds.

"Hang on, there, girl." Dr. Eastman's soothing voice penetrated my foggy brain. His warm hand held the back of my head and his arm and shoulder pressed into my back as he sat down next to me, propping me up.

"Geez, Delaney. I know the expression is melt to the floor, but I've never actually seen anyone look like they could do that." Daphne stood behind the paramedic watching the action.

What was she talking about? I was melting? I wasn't hot.

"Why am I not surprised it's you who's involved in this?"

My head lolled forward at the sound of Jack's deep voice. I frowned as his words registered. "'S'not my fault. Car… tried to…" I lifted my good arm and flipped my fingers from the street to the sidewalk.

He frowned and looked at Daphne. "She okay?"

"She's high." A smirk flirted with Daphne's face. "They gave her morphine." She nodded to the paramedics.

"It's good stuff," I muttered. "I feel no pain."

Lindsay chuckled. "That's good, because we're about to move your arm."

A bit of my brain fog disappeared, and I frowned. "How about no?"

"Unfortunately, we need to. Your distal pulse is weak, so the blood flow has been compromised."

An alarm bell clanged distantly in my head. I knew that was bad, but I also couldn't grasp why.

"We'll try to be quick." Lindsay patted my arm. "Tom, are you ready?" She turned to her partner.

He held up a splint. "Let's do this."

She nodded once, then looked at the pharmacist. "Dr. Eastman, if you could hold her steady, that would be great."

"Of course." He shifted, wrapping an arm securely around my body.

"Okay, Delaney. Here we go."

As my sluggish brain tried to process Lindsay's words, a sharp pain pierced my arm. I cried out as I felt the bones scrape together. Lindsay's hands pressed against my arm, manipulating things into place. In moments, my arm was straight, and Tom had the splint under it.

Breathing hard, I looked at them through watery and blurry eyes. "Ow."

"Sorry, hon." Lindsay gave me a sympathetic smile. "It's straight now, though. Once the throbbing dies down, it should feel much better."

It already did. Only a dull ache remained. I sagged into Dr. Eastman's hold, letting the morphine take over again. My eyes slid shut.

"Are you sure she's all right?" I heard Jack ask.

"She's fine," Lindsay replied. "We just gave her *a lot* of morphine. That's a nasty break."

"My cookies…" I muttered, once again lamenting the fact I wouldn't be baking for a while.

"What cookies?" Darcy asked.

"Can't bake. So no cookies." I blinked slowly at my sister.

"Let's worry about your arm right now. We'll figure out the cookies later."

I groaned. I didn't want to worry about any of it. I just wanted my problems to magically disappear.

Stupid car…

"Can someone tell me what happened?" Jack asked. "The only report I've heard is attempted hit and run."

"We were waiting to cross the street," Daphne said.

"Because ice cream," I inserted, looking up at him. "You're so pretty."

His lips twitched. "Thank you."

Confusion drew my eyebrows together. Why was he thanking me?

Two seconds later, realization dawned.

I groaned. "Oh no. I said that out loud, didn't I?"

He chuckled. "You did."

"Crud," I muttered. "Great job, Laney. Let the hot cop know how you feel."

"Delaney." Darcy whispered loudly. "You're still talking out loud."

I groaned again and covered my face with my good hand. "Just bury me alive. Right now." I no longer liked the morphine. It took away the stop-gap between my brain and my mouth. I wanted it back.

Daphne chuckled. "No need for that. I'm sure he understands you're just a teensy bit loopy at the moment."

I peeked through my fingers at her. "Seriously?" She had to be kidding.

Grinning, she nodded. "Anyway," She turned her attention to Jack. "Yes. We were on our way to get ice cream. While waiting for the light to change, we heard a squeal of tires coming from that way." She pointed around the corner to the left. "I looked up and saw the car coming at us. Delaney grabbed my arm and pulled me back."

"She dove into me," Darcy said. "Which is probably how she broke her arm. She didn't have any hands free to break her fall. I landed on my back."

"And I landed on my side and partly on top of her." Daphne nodded at me.

"But she pulled me out of the way." Darcy's voice grew thick. "I wasn't watching. If she hadn't tackled me—" She broke off with a shaky breath.

"Okay, what did the vehicle look like?"

"Black. Big," I said.

"Yeah. It was a big black SUV. A Chevy maybe? Or a GMC? It as big and boxy. I'm not good with cars." Daphne waved a hand. "But there was a woman driving. Blonde, from what I could see. And she had on oversize sunglasses."

"You're welcome to check my cameras, Detective," Dr. Eastman said. "I have one that points toward the street. It might have caught a license plate."

"Sounds good, thank you. We'll look just as soon as Delaney's loaded into the ambulance." Jack nodded to me.

"Which will be right now." Lindsay got to her feet. "We're ready to go."

"I don't think I can walk." I blinked several times,

attempting to bring her into focus. "The world is on a tilt-a-whirl."

She smiled. "That's why Tom went to get the chair."

"He did?" I raised my head, looking around. Tom was on his way back from the ambulance with a folded rolling chair. "Oh. Cool."

When he reached us, he quickly unfolded it and unlatched the buckles. With Lindsay and Dr. Eastman's help, I made it onto the padded seat without falling over. The paramedics strapped me in, then made the world tilt violently as they tipped me back to wheel me to the ambulance.

I closed my eyes as a wave of nausea hit me and prayed hard that my dinner stayed down.

Maybe morphine wasn't all it was cracked up to be.

Nineteen

"I cannot believe you still insist on going to Seattle." Mom propped her hands on her hips and glared at me as I packed my suitcase one-handed.

"What else am I supposed to do?" I asked, dumping a handful of rolled socks into the bag.

"Oh, I don't know. Stay home and rest?" She gave me a pointed look.

I rolled my eyes. "Then I'll just stress about my bakery business. The only saving grace is I don't have any building or staff overhead to worry about." My truck was paid off—thankfully—which was a relief. My house, however, was not. Nor was my personal vehicle. But, so long as I could fulfill my wedding contracts for the next few weeks and work the festival, I wouldn't default on either of those. Plus, I had my savings I could dip into if I truly had to.

Which I really didn't want to do. My hope was once the orthopedic surgeon put my arm back together, I'd have enough mobility to get back in the kitchen. But that wouldn't happen until Monday.

The last two days were a blur. Partly because of the pain meds and partly because a lot had happened. Once the paramedics transported me to the hospital, the ER staff examined and x-rayed my arm, discovering two fractures to my ulna, one in the rounded part of the joint and another in the long bone. The olecranon—the rounded part—fracture was stable, but the other one needed to be plated. Yesterday, I had a consultation with the surgeon, who put me in a temporary cast, then scheduled me for surgery.

"I told you not to stress about it. Your dad and I can help you out. Both in the kitchen and financially if you need it."

For which I was grateful. But that didn't mean I wasn't still worried. My business was a full-time job. So was my parents' inn. It wouldn't be as simple as Mom made it seem.

"Yes, well, the stressing will still happen. And we don't have time to put off Daphne's dress. I will be a passenger princess the whole way there and back. It's not like we're going hiking up a mountain or something. We'll be walking through Seattle. Or on public transport. I'll be fine." I crossed to my blonde maple dresser for a handful of underwear.

Mom shifted her weight and crossed her arms. "I still don't like it. You're vulnerable like that."

"I was unbroken *here* and this still happened." I gestured to my arm, a pile of panties in my hand. "I'm not worried." I threw the underwear on top of my other clothes, then flipped the lid shut. Grasping the zipper, I tried to yank it closed, but the lid wouldn't stay still. After several tries, I growled at it, then let go with a huff.

"See? You can't even close your suitcase on your own."

"But I have figured out how to get dressed without help and take a shower. This is nothing." To prove my point, I turned and sat on it, then gave the zipper another yank. That got it started, and I quickly had it far enough around that I could stand up and zip it the rest of the way.

Mom sighed. "You always were the most stubborn."

I flashed her a quick smile. "That's because I'm the most sensible."

She snorted, then laughed. "No."

She was right. Daphne was. That was the curse of being the eldest. But I wasn't far behind.

"So, will you drive me over to Daphne's now?" The plan was for the three of us to meet at her house after lunch, which was now. We wanted to be on the road by one. That would put us in the city just before rush hour.

Mom pursed her lips and stared at me for several seconds. But finally, she nodded. "Fine. But please take breaks?"

"I will. And I have my pain pills and reusable ice packs. I'm not unprepared."

"Good." She reached for my suitcase. "I still plan to warn your sisters to watch out for you, though."

I smiled, feeling loved, even though she was bordering on treating me like a child. She was worried, and I would always be her baby. "I'm sure you will."

After giving Millie a healthy dose of cuddles and scratches —Mom would come feed her every day and spend some time with her—we left.

Daphne's house, like most other things in Fernwood, wasn't far away. Seven minutes after leaving my little cottage, we pulled up to her pale gray single-story modern farmhouse. Mom parked behind Darcy's car on the street. We were taking Daphne's vehicle. Originally, we planned to take mine since it was the newest and the roomiest, but hers was only a couple of years older and not much smaller. It would be fine for the three of us.

Mom grabbed my suitcase from the back of her car, then we headed up the walkway and went inside.

"Knock, knock," Mom called.

"Hey." Daphne looked up from the kitchen island off to the right. A plate with a sandwich and fruit sat in front of her. "I'm almost ready. My bag is packed."

"Where's Darcy?" I glanced around, but didn't see her.

"Putting her bag in the car. She should be in soon."

Five seconds later, the interior door to the garage opened and Darcy stepped through.

"I thought I heard a car outside." She smiled at us, then settled her gaze on me. "How's the arm?"

"It's fine."

Mom snorted. "She hurts. Don't let her lie."

I rolled my eyes. "Of course it's sore. It's broken. But I'm *fine*." I was beginning to rethink my decision to let her and Dad help with my business. She'd probably just fret until my cast came off. Scarlett would probably help. In fact, she already offered when I told her about what happened.

Mom held up her hands. "So you've said." She glanced at Daphne and Darcy. "Keep an eye on her. Don't let her overdo it."

"We won't, Mom. She'll be okay." Daphne offered her a reassuring smile.

But still, she didn't look entirely convinced. She didn't argue, though.

"Do you three need anything else before I go back to the inn?"

"No, I think we're good," Daphne replied. She caught my gaze, and I gave her a smile of thanks. I loved my mother, but I was ready for her to not hover anymore.

"All right. Please let me know when you get there."

"We will." Daphne speared a strawberry and ate it.

"Okay. Have a safe trip. And have fun." She walked forward and gave Daphne a squeeze. "I wish I could come with you. But it's been the wedding season from hell for the inn."

Daphne hugged her back. "I know. But we'll put you up on the big screen. You'll be right there with us."

"And I will lock myself in my office so I'm sure not to be interrupted." Kissing Daphne's cheek, Mom stepped back. "Okay, I'll see you girls when you get back. *Be careful.*"

"We will," the three of us chorused.

Waving her fingers, Mom left.

Daphne shoveled the last of her food into her mouth and got up. "M'kay. I'm ready." Depositing her dishes in the dishwasher, she refilled her water bottle, and we traipsed out to the garage. Darcy stowed my suitcase in the back next to hers, then we piled into the car and were on our way.

The first hour of the drive we spent in casual conversation and letting the stress of our lives melt away with the miles. Even the impending surgery to fix my arm seemed like a distant task.

But the ding of Daphne's phone brought some of the tension back to her shoulders when she glanced at the screen.

"Everything okay, Daph?"

She met my gaze in the rearview mirror. "It's fine. Morgan's just having a bad day. I don't know what happened now. I'll look at it when we stop." She readjusted her grip on the steering wheel.

"Do you want me to drive?" Darcy asked.

"No. It's fine. Honestly, I'd rather not talk to him. Not about that."

I frowned. "What? Why not? Are you guys having trouble?"

"No. It's just—" She broke off and heaved a sigh. "I'm tired of hearing about Phil. It's been nothing but drama since he died, and Morgan's right in the middle of it. So, of course, he brings it home. Which I get. You should be able to rant to your partner. But it's been a little much. Every day, there's some new crisis."

"Like what? I mean, I know Mandi quit, but what else has happened?" I sat forward. Had Morgan or someone else at the office uncovered a clue about why Phil was murdered? Or about who could have motive?

"More of the same, really. Just chaos. People calling, worried about their cases and legal paperwork. With Mandi gone, there's no one to answer the phone and pass along messages, so they're taking turns trying to do their own work while they man the front desk. It hasn't been easy. And this morning, Morgan texted me and said Nile took off."

"Took off?" Darcy said. "Like, just left for the day or disappeared?"

"Both. He said he left and now won't answer his phone."

"Maybe the grief has finally caught up with him," I reasoned. "Phil was his friend, not just his partner."

"Yeah." Daphne glanced at her phone in the center console, then turned back to the road. "Maybe."

"You don't sound convinced." My frown turned thoughtful. "Why not?"

She lifted one shoulder. "Because I don't think they were really friends."

I blinked twice. That was news to me. "Isn't that why he moved here? To set up a law practice with his friend, Phil?"

"That's what they've said, yes. But Morgan said they'd been arguing a lot. It was always behind closed doors, and he couldn't really make out what they were saying, but he could hear raised voices."

"Hmm." I sat back and looked out my window. That was interesting. No one had mentioned Phil and Nile were at odds. But considering the way most everyone else viewed Phil Brunswick—including his own sister—I shouldn't be surprised.

"Were there any big cases they were working on together?" Darcy shifted, resting an elbow on the center arm rest so she could better see us both.

"Not that I know of." Daphne glanced at her. "But Morgan didn't talk about work. At least, not the cases or his clients. He couldn't. But I haven't gotten the sense there was anything particularly large brewing at the office. Just your normal stuff. Wills, some court cases, a few real estate things." She shrugged again. "I don't know. It's all just... crazy and bizarre. And I want it to be over. Can we talk about something else?"

"Of course." Darcy patted her knee. "What are we going to do with Delaney for the holiday now that she can't swim?" She sent me a side-eye smile.

One side of my mouth lifted, but I didn't respond. My mind was too busy wondering what Phil and Nile had to argue over.

Their law practice?

Maybe it was failing, and they didn't want anyone to know. They employed several lawyers, plus Mandi. Perhaps there wasn't enough business to keep everyone employed.

A case?

It was possible they were working on something the others didn't know about, and they couldn't agree on how to handle it. Or maybe the client was a real bear to work with, and only one of them wanted to drop the client.

Or it could be something personal.

But what?

Borrowed money?

I wrinkled my nose. No. I doubted that was the case. Judging by the house I'd been in, and the comments Skyler Brunswick-Taft made, Phil wasn't hurting for money. I doubted Nile was, either. Their income was similar.

But if it wasn't money, what could it be? A woman, maybe? Even though they were both married?

Maybe it was some other kind of business deal. One that didn't have anything to do with the law. Perhaps they'd invested in something and it went belly up.

"Earth to Delaney."

Darcy's voice penetrated my musings. I glanced up. "What?"

"We asked how your boyfriend was doing." A devilish smile lit her face.

"Very funny." I rolled my eyes. Sometimes, my sisters were still teenagers.

She and Daphne both chuckled.

"You did call him pretty." Daphne smiled at me through the mirror.

I huffed. "I was high on morphine. And he is. It was an honest slip of the tongue." I still couldn't believe I'd said that out loud and in front of him. The next time I had to take morphine, I'd steer well-clear of him.

Darcy hummed. "Sure. Keep telling yourself that."

"He seemed quite amused—and dare I say enamored with you?" Daphne said.

"You're delusional. Amused, yes. Enamored? Well, you're probably confusing that with the way someone looks at a person they find freakishly entertaining." I'd done nothing but put my foot in my mouth around Jack Fiore. There was no way he was enamored with me. He probably saw me as some sort of sideshow.

Both women laughed.

"I wouldn't say that." Darcy's gaze met mine.

"I would. Let's change the subject again. To your love life. How's that going?" I aimed a sickly-sweet smile at her.

Her smile only widened. "It's nonexistent, which I'm fine with."

"Of course you are," I muttered, looking out the window again.

Darcy turned to Daphne. "When we get back, we should go have a chat with Tyson Harris. Convince him to ask Laney out."

An exasperated sigh left my lungs, and I closed my eyes. Maybe if I feigned sleep for the rest of the drive, they'd leave me alone.

"Good plan. We could go talk to the hunky detective too."

I clenched my teeth. They'd better not. I'd whip out the

embarrassing pictures I had from high school and put them on a slideshow for Daphne's wedding if she dared.

Despite my intent to feign sleep, soon, real sleep slowly pulled at the edges of my brain. I might have insisted to Mom that I was fine, but my body knew something was wrong.

So, I didn't fight it. As my sisters chatted in the front seat, I let sleep pull me in and drifted off to the memory of kind, warm brown eyes set into a handsome, smiling face as I sat, high as a kite, on the bench in front of Eastman's Pharmacy.

Twenty

"Should we whisper?" I looked up at the crystal chandeliers illuminating the Peabody Gallery as we walked inside. "I feel like we should whisper." Warm light bounced off the stark white walls, which were interspersed with brightly colored paintings and vivid photographs. Gleaming maple wood floors stretched beneath our feet. "This is definitely a place you whisper."

Daphne chuckled softly. "For sure."

Darcy waved a hand at us. "You're being ridiculous."

I arched an eyebrow at her, noting that she, too, kept her voice low.

With a huff, she walked away, portfolio tucked under arm as she headed deeper into the gallery.

I looked at Daphne, my eyebrow still raised.

"She must really want this," she muttered.

"I guess so." I tipped my head toward Darcy. "Come on."

We caught up as she approached a woman about our age dressed in a black pencil skirt, black heels, a lavender top, and a tan three-quarter-sleeve blazer.

"Hello." Darcy held out a hand to the woman. "My name

is Darcy Fowler. I called earlier this week and set up an appointment with Ms. Peabody to look at my portfolio."

The woman, who was also on the tall side, tipped her chin up and looked down her nose at Darcy. "Ms. Peabody doesn't take cold calls for prospective artists."

The polite smile on Darcy's face took on a strained note. I clenched my good hand into a fist by my side and forced my expression to stay neutral. Someone needed to tell this woman she wasn't any better than the rest of us just because she worked in some lofty art gallery.

"Well, she made an exception for me for some reason, because I'm on her schedule. How about you go look?"

With a soft harrumph, the woman spun on her heel and marched away.

"Do you think she'll actually check?" Daphne peered around Darcy, watching the woman saunter toward the rear of the gallery.

"Probably not," Darcy grumbled. "Let's follow."

She took off before Daphne or I could say a word.

"Mom told us to be careful, but she forgot to warn us not to do anything dumb," I muttered.

Daphne chuckled under her breath. "Because she knows she'd be talking to the air."

I grinned. "True." I quickened my pace to keep up with Darcy.

We stayed well behind the woman, pretending to look at the art when she glanced back just before she walked through a door marked "Staff Only."

After waiting about thirty seconds, we wandered over there at Darcy's insistence.

"What do you plan to do?" Daphne asked.

In answer, Darcy tried the door handle. It turned beneath her palm.

Daphne grabbed her forearm as she pushed the door inward. "We can't go in there!" she hissed.

"You can stay out here, but I'm not going to let her ruin my chance to be featured in this gallery. Coral was interested in the pictures I emailed her. That's how I got the meeting. I refuse to leave without at least talking to her." Eyes glittering with determination and her mouth set in a firm line, she pushed the door open.

Daphne sent me a quick panicked look, her eyes as round as giant gumballs, and hurried in after her.

I sighed and followed. This was such a bad idea, but I saw Darcy's point. And honestly, bad ideas had never stopped us before.

The corridor was quiet. More art lined the white walls between closed doors, and a few potted plants took up space near the end of the hallway, where it turned to the right and disappeared.

"Where did she go?" Daphne whispered.

"I don't know," Darcy replied. "Let's see if we can find Coral's office."

"What are you going to say when you knock? It's not like anyone told you to come back here." I took careful steps so my shoes wouldn't echo on the floor. Though, I wasn't sure why. Our whispers echoed down the hall. We weren't exactly being stealthy.

"I don't know." Darcy glanced back. "I'll probably just say I didn't see anyone out there, so I decided to take a chance. Maybe she'll appreciate my moxie."

"Or she'll call security on us." Daphne's eyes had yet to return to their normal shape.

We passed two doors before coming upon one with a gold placard that had Coral's name etched into it.

"Here goes nothing." Darcy raised her fist to knock. But just before her hand made contact, she paused and leaned forward, turning her head.

"What?" I frowned. Why wasn't she knocking?

Darcy flapped a hand, then laid a finger over her lips.

I sidled closer. So did Daphne.

That's when I heard it. A woman's voice. And only one. She must be on the phone.

"I don't care, Gage." The woman's voice rose. "You need to come home. Before this blows up in your face. Yves said—" She stopped.

Yves said what? Who was Gage, and what was she talking about? Before what blew up in his face? I leaned closer.

"Fine. Do what you want," she snapped.

We heard a soft clatter, then nothing.

"Did she hang up?" I mouthed to my sisters.

Darcy shrugged. We all took a step back.

That turned out to be a good thing. A few seconds later, the door opened.

Coral Peabody paused in the doorway, surprise on her perfectly made-up face. A frown quickly descended. "Who are you? Why are you back here? This area is off-limits to guests."

"Sorry." Darcy raised her hands. "I have an appointment with you. Darcy Fowler. We spoke to one of your employees in the gallery, but she didn't seem keen on informing you I was here. When you didn't come out, we poked our heads back here and didn't see anyone."

I was glad to hear her stick closer to the truth. The walls had eyes in the form of cameras. It would be easy to verify— or debunk—her story.

Coral's frown smoothed out slightly, and she released a short sigh. "Kayleigh guards me like a rottweiler. Let's go down to the conference room, shall we?" She motioned to the left, back the way we'd come.

We moved back enough for her to exit her office and close the door. She led us down the hall and through the door to the gallery. From there, we stuck close to the rear wall until we reached a room with a wall of windows. Through them, I saw a long table ringed with comfortable chairs.

"We'll wait out here." I grabbed Daphne's arm, keeping her from following Darcy and Ms. Peabody inside. This was Darcy's meeting. She didn't need us there hovering or advocating for her. I knew my sister and the beauty in her art. Her work would speak for itself.

Daphne glanced back with a frown, then nodded. She turned to Darcy. "We'll be wandering."

While Coral closed the door, Daphne and I meandered toward the nearest display. A bronze sculpture of an eye set atop a sphere.

"Some art is just… strange." She tipped her head, staring at the piece.

"Yeah." I gave it a quick glance, not too interested in it. My mind was still running through what we overheard. I really wanted to know what Yves said to Coral.

My mouth flattened. I needed to let it go. It was highly unlikely I'd ever find out. I couldn't just walk up to her and ask. She'd know we were eavesdropping, and I didn't want to jeopardize Darcy's chances of exhibiting at the gallery.

Trying to shake off my thoughts, I turned and wandered toward the paintings on the wall. As I cleared a sleek statue of a woman holding a flower to the sky, the front door opened. I glanced over and saw a man enter.

One I recognized.

I ducked behind the statue. This was not good. "Daphne! Psst!"

She turned, frowning. "Why are you hiding?"

I patted the air. "Keep your voice down!" I hissed.

"Why?" she asked, softer.

I pointed toward the door.

She looked over. I knew the moment she saw who I'd seen. Her eyes rounded, and she stepped back, moving behind a wide ceramic vase on a pedestal.

"Oh boy."

"Right?" I closed my eyes, swallowing a groan. "What is he *doing* here?" Easing forward, I peered around the statue.

Right into Jack Fiore's eyes.

Twenty-One

With a squeak, I ducked behind the statue again, but it was too late. He'd seen me.

Crap!

"He's coming this way," Daphne whispered.

I couldn't hold back the groan this time. Of all the people to show up when we were here, why him?

A wall of muscled man in a black jacket, gray shirt, and jeans appeared in front of me.

I kept my eyes on his chest, hoping he'd look right over me and keep walking.

"Delaney."

Rats!

I clenched my good fist and lifted my gaze, pasting a sunny smile of surprise on my face. "Jack. Hi. Fancy meeting you here."

His dark eyebrows dipped low over his equally dark eyes. "Right? Crazy coincidence." He crossed his arms, the glower still in full effect. "Why are you here?"

"It's not what you think." I raised my hand, warding off the accusations I could see in his eyes.

"Really? Because it looks like you're meddling in my investigation. Again."

"We're not, I promise."

His frown turned curious. "We?"

"My sisters are here too." I looked past his shoulder, where Daphne still stood by the vase.

He glanced back, then around the gallery. His posture turned rigid when he saw Darcy in the conference room with Coral. "Why is she talking to Coral Peabody?" He turned an accusatory look on me. "Did you put her up to that? I told you not to get involved."

Indignation straightened my spine. "I would never ask my sisters to do what I'm capable of doing myself." My face colored as I basically admitted to poking my nose where it didn't belong. I waved a hand. "Not that we're meddling. Darcy's an artist. A good one. She scheduled a meeting with Ms. Peabody to discuss having some of her work featured here. That's what they're talking about. Daphne and I tagged along because we're going wedding dress shopping after this."

He turned, looking through the windows again to study the pair. "So, it's purely coincidence you three are here now?"

I lifted a shoulder. "Yes." Mostly.

Jack returned his attention to me. Skepticism still lingered in his gaze. "You've had this planned for a while?"

I glanced away, shrugging once more.

"Mmm," he hummed. "So, not all coincidence."

"I needed to shop for a wedding dress." Daphne walked over to stand beside me. "Darcy took advantage of that and scheduled her meeting. That Coral's boat is part of your homicide investigation *is* coincidental."

I wagged a finger at him. "But we did learn something."

His eyes narrowed. "I knew you were snooping."

"It wasn't intentional," Daphne said, defending me.

"It wasn't," I agreed. "Her assistant is a—well, you know. A b-word." I flip-flopped my good hand. "Anyway, she didn't want to inform Coral that Darcy was here to see her, so we snuck into the back."

"Of course you did." He huffed. "Go on."

"We were about to knock when Darcy heard Coral talking in her office. It sounded like she was on the phone to someone named Gage."

Jack's gaze sharpened. "You're sure it was Gage?"

I shared a look with Daphne, then nodded. "Yes. Why?"

"What did she say?" he asked, ignoring my question.

"She told him to come home before 'this'"—I air-quoted—"blew up in his face. She started to say something about Yves but stopped. Then a few seconds later, she told him to do what he wanted and hung up."

He turned slightly, looking back at the conference room again, chewing on the corner of his mouth.

"Who's Gage?" I asked again.

"Her son."

"Her—" I broke off, and my eyes widened as realization dawned. "Was he the one driving the boat?"

He met my gaze but stayed silent.

I pressed my lips together. "Okay. I guess that's privileged information." I rocked back on my heels, then decided to ask another question. "Did you talk to Yves?"

Again, he held my gaze but stayed silent.

My jaw worked, and I tried again. "Why are you here? You couldn't talk to her over the phone?" I nodded toward the conference room.

"In-person interviews are generally better. I can't read body language over a phone line."

"He speaks!" A smile pulled at my mouth.

"Funny."

I chuckled. "I thought so."

He lifted his arm and checked the watch on his wrist, then glanced at the conference room.

"Don't you dare interrupt them." I moved to stand between him and the door. "Let Darcy have her meeting. Waiting a few minutes isn't going to make or break your investigation."

"It will if she asks questions she shouldn't. Like you do."

It was my turn to stay silent. I couldn't promise him Darcy wouldn't say something. I didn't think she would simply because it could make Coral change her mind about featuring Darcy's work. But Darcy didn't always think through the words that left her mouth.

So, I said a silent prayer she'd stick to business.

Ten agonizing minutes passed. Jack's impatience increased with every glance at his watch until I thought he'd just say screw it and interrupt them.

But fortunately, they finished their meeting and Darcy exited the room, excitement shining in the barely suppressed smile on her face. Ms. Peabody held two rolled up canvases.

"Thank you for your time, Ms. Peabody. I'll email you pictures of my other paintings just as soon as I can." Tucking her portfolio under her arm, she hurried over to us.

Her step faltered for half a second when she saw Jack, but she quickly recovered. "Well, hello, Detective."

Coral's face tensed.

Jack's expression tightened, and he stepped around Darcy. "Excuse me."

Darcy turned, frowning, then looked at me and Daphne. "What did I say?"

"He's here to talk to her about her boat." I moved closer, watching his interaction with Coral. The older woman led him into the conference room and shut the door.

"Should we wait, or just leave?" Darcy asked.

"We need to go. My appointment at the bridal salon is in

thirty minutes. I doubt he'll be very forthcoming with information, anyway. Delaney tried, and he just gave her the stink eye."

Darcy turned to me with a wicked smile. "Trouble in paradise?"

I sighed and spun on my heel. "Don't even start. Let's go."

Twenty-Two

Fiery shards of pain throbbed through my arm as I settled onto the bed in my hotel room, ready to watch an hour or so of television before I crashed for the night. Even though it would have been cheaper—and heaven knew I needed to save every penny I could right now—my sisters and I opted for separate rooms. We all liked our space, and someone would have been the odd girl out, since there were only two beds. Plus, with my arm, I didn't really want to share a bed. If anyone was going to jostle it in the night, it would be me.

I picked up the remote and flicked on the TV, scrolling through the menu that popped up. Maybe there was a fun Hallmark movie on. I could go for a little romance. Dress shopping with Daphne had put me in the mood for love. When we'd flipped through gowns, I'd seen several I liked. But for me, not her. I hadn't really wanted to analyze what that meant at the time, but alone in the shower just a little bit ago, I realized that perhaps I was more ready for a long-term relationship than I thought.

I shoved that line of thinking away. That was for another day. When I wasn't in pain or feeling lonely because my sister was in the throes of love.

The line for the Hallmark channel popped up on the screen. I did a mental fist pump when I saw a movie listed. It was one I'd watched before and liked. Clicking on it, I adjusted the volume, then set the remote on the nightstand. I was ready to not move. The painkiller I took before I got in the shower needed to kick in. I'd held the worst of the pain at bay all day with ibuprofen, but all the moving around and walking had taken a toll. I finally gave in and took something stronger. There was already a nice fuzziness descending. Soon, the more severe pain would fade, and I would be able to sleep. I hoped.

A soft knock sounded on the hotel room door. I turned my head to stare at it with a frown. I really didn't want to get up. I said goodnight to both of my sisters after they helped me take off my shirt and wrap my arm in plastic wrap so I could shower.

I eyed my phone, debating texting them to find out who it was and what she wanted.

Another knock sounded. This time, a masculine voice followed. "Delaney? It's Jack."

My eyes widened. What was he doing here? Better yet, how did he find me?

Sitting up, I swung my legs over the side of the bed, wincing as the movement jostled my arm. The pain was better, but not gone yet.

My bare feet padded softly on the carpet as I crossed the room. Unlocking the deadbolt, I swung the door open.

All six-feet-two inches of Jack Fiore stood on the other side. Black beard stubble dusted his strong jaw, giving him a more casual look. The thigh-hugging jeans and black jacket that emphasized his broad shoulders only added to his appeal.

Why did he have to be so darned handsome? He would never give me the time of day. Men like him dated women who looked like supermodels, not averagely built bakers who usually had a streak of flour on their faces and detested high heels. And until I could shake this crazy attraction to him, dating anyone else would be pointless.

So, I frowned up at him. "Jack? What are you doing here? How did you even find me?"

He stared at me for a long moment, his dark eyes raking over my pajama-clad body.

Heat licked at my cheeks, but not from desire. It was a blush of embarrassment. I forgot I'd only put on a thin tank top after my shower. T-shirt sleeves were too much without help. The tank had spaghetti straps I could stretch over the arm wrapped at a ninety-degree angle. My more *womanly assets* were covered but not well.

I crossed my broken arm across my chest and set the other one over top. At least I had on pants and not the booty shorts that went with the top.

Jack cleared his throat and met my gaze. "Sorry. I didn't know you'd be ready for bed this early."

"It's fine. What can I do for you?"

"I wanted to ask you a couple of questions. About Gage Peabody."

"I don't know him."

His brows knit together. "At all? He spends a decent amount of time in Fernwood."

Stepping back, I motioned him inside, figuring we should have this conversation in private.

Not that anyone walking past would know who or what we were talking about. It just felt weird to discuss a murder investigation where strangers could hear.

He entered my room and closed the door, but didn't move further inside.

"I've probably seen him around town, but I don't know what he looks like," I said.

Jack took his phone from his pocket. He tapped the screen several times, then turned it around. "This is Gage."

I looked at the picture, recognition dawning when I saw the smiling man with wavy light-brown hair. "Okay. I stand corrected. I do know him. Not well, but he's stopped at my food truck a few times during festivals and such. He likes my sugar cookies." I tipped my head, remembering something that happened a few weeks prior. "And he asked me once if I made anything gluten and sugar free. Said his girlfriend didn't eat either."

"Did you see the girlfriend?"

"No. He was alone."

"Why did that interaction stick with you? I mean, people must ask you stuff like that all the time."

"It happens, yes. But on that particular occasion I found it odd because there was another truck there that only sold gluten-free. And they had a lot of sugar-free stuff too. It was just a few spots down from me. It was at the town's Memorial Day celebration. When I asked if he'd tried their truck, he said not yet. That he was hoping I'd have something because he liked my cookies so much." I lightly shrugged my good shoulder. "I thought it was a nice compliment."

A slight frown wrinkled my forehead. "Why are you asking about him? What did Coral tell you? Is he the one who drove the boat?"

"I can't tell you any of that. I just need to know what you know about him. Is he in Fernwood often?"

"I really don't know. You'd be better off asking some of the vacationers. They socialize with each other more than they do with us locals."

"Obviously, they socialize with the locals some if Felicity Brunswick was with one of them."

It wasn't an admission, but the tone of his voice and the look in his eyes suggested he meant Gage. I couldn't stop myself from calling him on it. "So it *was* Gage on the boat." I moved my arms away from my chest and raised a finger.

Air-conditioned air whispered over me. Goosebumps tightened my skin and other… areas.

Feeling the flush of embarrassment again, I spun around and marched toward my suitcase, plucking my lightweight cotton robe off the top. Swinging it over my left shoulder, I tried to keep it over my arm while I fished behind my back for the right sleeve.

Jack walked over to stand in front of me. He reached around my back and held the robe open.

"Thank you." I slid my right arm in the sleeve and glanced up at him through my lashes.

"You're welcome." His deep voice held a gruff note.

I clutched the robe together near my neck.

"How's the arm?" He motioned to the bandaged appendage now hiding behind the light blue fabric.

"Broken. But it doesn't hurt too much," I fibbed. "I took some stronger painkillers just a little while ago." They were definitely helping now. The pain had receded some.

A small smile graced his sculpted lips. "That would explain the slightly glassy look in your eyes. Though it's not as bad as it was the last time I saw you."

My mouth tilted up. "Yeah, the tablets aren't quite as strong as the IV stuff."

"When do you get it set in a proper cast?"

"Monday. They're going to insert a plate and some screws."

He winced. "Ouch. I can't believe you're here when you're facing that yet."

"It's provided a nice distraction. Plus, Daphne can't really afford to delay any of her preparations. Not if she wants to stick to her wedding date."

"What's the rush?"

"A desire to not be engaged for over a year. She's determined to have a fall wedding."

"Ah. That makes sense. I wouldn't want that long of an

engagement, either. I don't know how people do it. But then, I don't want a huge wedding like some do."

Did that mean he had a woman in his life who also felt that way? "And how does your girlfriend feel about that?"

"I don't have one. But if I did, I suppose we'd have to come up with a compromise on wedding size if we got that far. I doubt most women are like your sister."

I hummed. "You'd be surprised. There are more like her than you think." Feeling uncomfortable talking about weddings with the man likely to star in my dreams tonight, I changed the subject.

"How did you know where to look for me?"

"I, um, called your parents."

My eyes bugged. "You *what*?" I covered my face briefly. "Please tell me you gave them an explanation as to why you were looking for me? Because my mom will freak out and assume the worst."

He raised a hand. "Don't worry. I told them I ran into you three at the gallery and that I wanted to ask you a few follow-up questions."

"So they just gave you the name of our hotel and our room numbers, no questions asked?"

"Actually, your dad insisted on calling the police station to verify my cellphone number before he'd give me the information. I was pleased to hear him looking out for you."

I was happy to hear that too. I figured they wouldn't give that info out willy-nilly, but Mom was extra worried about us —about me—right now, so I wouldn't put it past her to blindly trust someone who said they were a cop and wanted to check on us.

"Well, good." I let my hand fall back to the neck of my robe, clutching it together again.

"I have another question for you."

"Oh? About Gage? I really don't know anything else about him."

"Not about Gage. About Yves."

I frowned. "What? Yves? What about him?"

"How well do you know him?"

My frown intensified. "We're not best friends, if that's what you're asking, but he's been my family's mechanic my entire life. And I guess you could consider him a family friend. He comes to some of the parties my parents throw."

"Okay. Personally, what do you know about him?"

"Personally? Why are you asking that? You can't possibly think he had anything to do with the Brunswicks' deaths. He wasn't even in town when Felicity died."

"Just answer the question, Delaney. You told me the other day he's dating Coral Peabody. What about other girlfriends? Does he have any children?"

"He's brought a few women to our family parties over the years, but not recently. As for kids, he's never mentioned any."

"Do you know where he's from originally? Because it's not Fernwood."

"It's not?" I didn't know he wasn't. He'd always been around, so I guess I just assumed he was.

"No."

"I don't know, then. My parents might. Or you could go ask Yves." Going straight to the source would probably be the wisest decision. I doubted Yves had anything to hide.

He made a noncommittal sound.

I tipped my head and studied him. "What do you know? And don't say nothing. Because you wouldn't be asking me these questions if there wasn't something."

Amusement danced in his eyes. "Don't ever let anyone tell you you're not perceptive. That said, I can't tell you. It's an active investigation."

A scowl darkened my face. "That is such crap. I did everything I could to save two people, and you won't even tell me who you suspect of murdering them. Or why."

The apologetic look he gave me rang false. Like he was sorry, but not.

"Again, it's an active investigation. I'm glad you did what you could to help them, but that doesn't change how I handle my investigation. There are some details I just can't give out." He narrowed his eyes. "And that doesn't mean you go back to Fernwood and start poking around, asking questions and trying to find out." He wagged a finger at me.

I resisted the urge to slap it away. Instead, I feigned an innocent look. "I would never." But if people talked to me while I sold them delicious baked goods, well, then, I wouldn't stop them.

"Delaney…" His voice held a note of warning, clearly not believing I wouldn't stick my nose where it didn't belong.

Maybe it was the medication making me angry with him for cutting me out. Or maybe it was just being used for information and given nothing in return. Likely, it was a combination of both. Either way, I pasted a sweet smile on my face and walked around him to the door, finished with the conversation. "I'm tired, Detective." Grasping the handle, I pulled it open. "I hope you find the answers you're looking for."

He stared at me, unmoving except for the muscle ticking in his jaw. After several seconds, he gave his head a soft shake and moved toward me. Pausing in the doorway, and so close I could smell the scent of the detergent he used wafting off his clothes, he turned those fathomless dark eyes on me.

"Please don't go home and ask questions. It's for your own good."

For my—

Anger erupted, swift and hot, in my belly at his patronizing tone. I was not a child who didn't know better. I had no intention of actively investigating Phil and Felicity's deaths. I wasn't an idiot.

Before I said something I'd regret, I gestured for him to exit. "Goodnight, Detective."

He held my gaze for another beat. "Goodnight, Ms. Fowler."

As soon as his backside cleared the threshold, I shut the door and threw the deadbolt.

His attitude had one positive effect: I was no longer enamored with his pretty eyes and movie star good looks.

The memory of his broad shoulders filling that black jacket flashed through my mind.

I clenched my teeth.

Mostly. I was mostly no longer enamored.

Twenty~Three

"There. Are you comfortable?" Mom fluffed my pillow and stepped back.

Slowly, I looked up at her, having learned my lesson about moving too fast when I got out of the car just a little while ago. I *did not* want the nausea to return. I'd nearly upchucked all over the inn's driveway. "I'm good."

"Do you need any more pain medicine?"

"No." I settled against the pillows and closed my eyes. "It's okay." I was pretty sure the nurses gave me all they could before we left the hospital, anyway. "I just want to sleep. Can you wake me when Scarlett arrives?" My best friend had volunteered to take over my food truck this week, but we needed to go over what needed to be done. This was the absolute worst timing for this injury. I didn't have a wedding to bake for, but I needed to bake several hundred cookies and cupcakes for the holiday festival this weekend. Normally, I'd offer cinnamon rolls, scones, and donuts too. Possibly even some cheesecake. But not this time. I just couldn't handle the variety with my injury.

"Are you sure you don't want to text her and ask her to come tomorrow?"

"Can't. If we don't start now, I won't be ready for Friday." I still had my eyes closed, but I could picture the scowl on Mom's face. "Scarlett's working for me when she's not at her boutique, so I only get her a few hours a day."

"The rest of us intend to help too."

"I know." I opened my eyes. "But you all have to work too. I'll be fine, so please don't worry. I just need to rest for a little while. Let the anesthesia wear off some."

She huffed. "You could at least move inside. You'll sleep better in a quiet room than out here." She gestured to the private deck where I sat on a lounger.

That's where she was wrong. There weren't many places I found more relaxing than the family's deck at the inn. It overlooked the lake and was off-limits to guests. They could still see me and talk to me from the ground if they truly wanted, but we had it roped off. Most everyone respected the signs proclaiming it for family access only.

"I'm fine." My eyelids slid shut.

Mom sighed. "All right. Well, you have your phone. If you need something, call me."

I nodded, eyes still closed. "Thanks, Mom."

"You're welcome, sweetie."

Moments later, I heard the soft thud of her shoes on the deck as she walked away.

I drifted off, but not to the peaceful sleep I'd hoped for. It wasn't fitful, but it wasn't the deep, deep sleep I wanted. Dreams plagued my unconscious mind, and several times, I stirred as one ended, the joyful shout of a child in the water or the bark of a dog pulling me from sleep.

When I heard footsteps approaching, my eyelids fluttered. My mind wanted to descend into sleep once more—even if it was full of crazy, weird dreams—but I knew it was probably Mom and Scarlett.

Sucking in a breath and stretching the best I could, I forced my eyes open.

But it wasn't Mom or Scarlett who stood at the end of my lounger.

"Yves?"

The glower on his face registered as I blinked away the sleep. Once it did, a sliver of unease went through me. So did the memory of Jack's questions Saturday evening. For the first time, I wondered if Yves was capable of hurting someone.

"You told Detective Fiore about me?"

My forehead wrinkled with confusion. "What? Told him what about you, exactly?"

"About my relationship with Coral."

"Yes. I told you it was important he know. Why are you angry? You gave Coral an alibi for Felicity's murder."

He propped his hands on his hips and looked away for several beats before aiming his dark look on me again. "Do you know what Detective Fiore's doing as we speak?"

The frown on my face grew deeper. "No. Should I?"

"He's arresting Coral's son for murder."

Twenty~Four

"Yves Taskin! Why are you up here bugging Delaney?"

I jumped at the sound of Mom's voice from the sliding door behind me to the right. Glancing over my shoulder, I saw her walk outside, gaze fixed on Yves.

"She's been meddling in what she doesn't understand."

"You're right. I don't," I said. "How about you enlighten me? How does me telling Jack about your relationship with Coral get her son arrested?"

"Because now Detective Fiore knows Gage was here alone and had access to the boat. He can't place anyone else on it."

"Okay. Did he murder Felicity?"

"No!"

I took a chance. "Did you?"

"No!" His voice increased in volume and took on a note of exasperation. Throwing a hand in the air, he let it fall to the top of his head and smoothed it over his silver hair as he spun to look out at the lake. Pacing to the railing, he stared at the water.

I shared a wide-eyed look with Mom.

She rolled her lips in, then took a step toward him. "Yves?"

His shoulders fell. "Gage didn't do it." He turned bleak eyes on us. "He loved her."

My eyes widened. I shared another surprised look with Mom. Yves turned and leaned against the railing, facing us.

"How about you start from the beginning, Yves?" Mom's soft tone seemed to calm his emotions some. His expression, though still pinched, looked a little less pained.

"Gage and Felicity have been together for nearly a year. He knew it was wrong, since she was married, but they"—he paused, drawing in a shaky breath—"they fell in love. Over an argument about the pitfalls of sugar." A soft smile tugged at his mouth.

"Sugar?" I asked.

He nodded. "Felicity was very health conscious. She was very careful about what she ate. Gage is not. They met at a party the Hudson's threw last year. Phil was out of town, and she came on her own. Anyway, he was eating sweet after sweet, and I guess he offered her one. She gave him a lecture on how bad she thought all that was for the human body, and they ended up in a long conversation. She just fascinated him."

I arched an eyebrow, but kept my mouth shut. Fascinating was the last word I would use to describe Felicity Brunswick. Several other rather rude words came to mind.

"Anyway, at first, he resisted. He knew she was married and didn't want to get involved with her because of that. But the more he saw of her and the more they talked, the more she got under his skin. Coral and I urged him to really think about what he was doing. Phil wasn't someone you trifled with. But it didn't matter. He fell in love." Yves looked out over the inn's grounds. "Anyway, about a month ago, Felicity finally told Gage she planned to divorce Phil. That she finally had 'what she needed' to get away from him." He made some quick air quotes with one hand.

"And what was that?" I asked.

He looked at me. "I don't know. But I got the feeling it was more than just money to live on."

"Does Gage know what it was?" Mom crossed her arms, curiosity pulling her eyebrows down.

"I think so, but he won't say what. At least, not to me or his mother. His lawyer is advising him not to say anything to anyone."

"What about the boat? Does he know who piloted it? Or why Felicity was on it?"

"No. That I know for sure, because I asked him point blank, and he denied knowing anything about it. He didn't even know the boat wasn't in its mooring at the house until the police showed up to ask him about it. And so far, the only usable prints they've found on it belong to him and Coral. And me."

That didn't sound right. "What about Felicity's? They didn't find hers?"

"Only on the railing outside. Where you said she collapsed."

I glanced at Mom, suspicion ringing alarm bells in my foggy brain. "That seems odd. She came from inside."

"I know." Yves held up his hands. "It's been wiped down. All the prints they took of us came from the cabins. The common areas and the pilothouse had been wiped clean."

"Well, that doesn't make sense," I said. "Why would Gage wipe those areas and not the rest of the boat? Why would he wipe them at all? It belongs to his family. His prints would be expected to be there."

"That's what I told Detective Fiore. But the evidence is pointing to Gage. He had motive and opportunity."

"What was his motive? Felicity said she was leaving her husband."

"That's the thing, though. The police haven't found any evidence she planned to divorce him." Yves ran a hand over the back of his head and gripped his neck. "They think Gage killed Phil, then killed Felicity. They're theorizing she dumped him after he killed Phil."

"With what evidence?" Mom asked. "They have to prove this in court."

"Yeah. But there's more." He paused, his gaze traveling from her to me, then back again. "Felicity was pregnant."

I blinked several times, suddenly unsure if I was awake or dreaming. "Come again?"

"Felicity and Gage were having a baby."

Mom shifted, uncrossing her arms and stuffing them in her back pockets. "Did Phil know? Was it possible he was blackmailing her?"

"Yes. That the police *did* find evidence of. I don't know where. They just said they have evidence Phil blackmailed them. He was threatening to kick Felicity out without a dime."

I frowned. "That doesn't make sense. Why threaten? She was carrying another man's baby. He had every reason to divorce her."

"Like I said, I think she had something on him. It left them at a stalemate."

"Did Coral know about this?" Mom asked softly. "Before the police, I mean?"

Yves looked at the ground, slowly nodding. "Yeah." He lifted his head. "Gage was pretty upset. Phil wouldn't grant Felicity a divorce, but she wouldn't back down. He and Coral had a long talk about it."

"Oh, Yves." Mom reached out and touched his arm.

A muscle ticked in Yves's jaw. He rolled his lips in, pressing them tightly together. "It's such a mess," he whispered. "But I know Gage. He didn't kill Phil. And he'd *never* hurt Felicity."

My mind whirled along, trying to process the information. It was hard to imagine anyone being enamored with Felicity, and even harder to think about her being a mother.

But one thing stuck out at me. If Gage didn't do it, who did?

"Yves? Who else could have known about Felicity and Gage?"

He crossed his arms, a slight furrow forming between his eyebrows. "I'm not sure, really. They tried not to make a spectacle out of it. I mean, they were seen together, talking at parties over the last year. But they never left together. They never went to restaurants together unless they were part of a group. They were careful. And it wasn't because they didn't want Phil to find out—he knew. He also had his own lady friend on the side. But they had an unspoken understanding that neither of them would embarrass the other."

"Which having a baby with another man would definitely do," Mom said.

Yves nodded. "Exactly." He turned to me. "I'm sorry, Delaney. I—I'm just… frustrated. Coral's upset because she can't be his alibi, and when she's upset it makes me upset. I know Detective Fiore would have eventually uncovered the truth about where she was, and that Gage was alone the day Felicity was murdered. You were just an easy target for my anger. I apologize."

"As you should," Mom admonished.

I raised my good hand. "Mom, it's okay." I looked at Yves. "I knew upsetting you was a possibility when I went to Jack with what you told me. But I couldn't hold back the information and still live with myself. Not if that information could lead to Felicity's killer."

"No, I understand." He offered me a tight smile. "Again, I'm sorry."

"It's already forgotten." I gave him a groggy smile, my energy levels flagging as the adrenaline that spiked during our conversation began to fade. "One question, though."

"What's that?"

"When are you and Coral getting married?"

Amusement sparked in his eyes. "What makes you think we will?"

"The way you talk about her. She means a lot to you."

His expression turned soft. "Yeah. She does. And to answer your question, I don't know. She likes Seattle. I like it here." He shrugged. "We're both old and set in our ways, so we'll see."

I smiled, looking up at him. "You're not so old."

Mom chuckled. "I'm glad you said that, because I'm not far off Yves's age."

Yves's smile blossomed. "But you look so much younger. That and the way you feel are what count." He took a step toward the stairs. "I should get going. I'm sorry again for my attitude." Backing away, he lifted a hand. "I hope your arm heals quickly, Delaney."

"Thank you."

Nodding once, he left.

Another set of footsteps echoed on the wooden stairs. As Yves disappeared, Scarlett ascended the steps to the deck.

She took in our somewhat flabbergasted expressions as she reached us, then glanced back with a frown toward where Yves just disappeared. "I feel like I missed something."

I barked a short laugh. "So much."

Twenty~Five

I took one last look around the church kitchen, making sure we had everything. My workspace was much more chaotic than usual. I loved my family and friends, but having all the extra hands in the kitchen had led to messy counters and ingredients not where they belonged. I didn't want anything to get missed.

But Scarlett and Darcy had scoured the counters and found it all. Not a forgotten tray was in sight.

Picking up my tote, I turned off the lights and headed upstairs, where they were loading the last of the goodies for the festival today. I couldn't believe we'd pulled it off.

I mean, I had hoped we would. Desperately. But I'd still had my doubts. It took me two days to muster enough energy and survive on non-narcotic pain medication so I could get back in the kitchen. But Scarlett and my family had taken my plans and run with them. I was so very thankful for all their help.

After locking the church doors, I stepped into the truck. All but a few boxes were put away. "You guys are seriously awesome. Thank you so much for helping." Nothing this week would have been possible without them.

Scarlett glanced over and grinned. "You're welcome. This is actually kind of fun. Don't get me wrong, I love being at my little store, but baking is a great stress reliever. Although"—she shook a finger at me—"I'm not a fan of the early mornings. But I'll do it for you."

A short chuckle escaped me. "I appreciate it."

"You're welcome."

I helped them put away the last few boxes, then hopped out to get in the passenger seat. Scarlett climbed in beside me. Darcy would follow in her car.

"I still can't believe we pulled this off," I said as we pulled onto the main road.

"I can. With all of us working, I never had any doubt."

Moisture gathered in my eyes. "I'm just so grateful. I don't know if my business would have survived without you all."

She sent me a sympathetic look. "Lucky for you, you don't have to worry about that. We'd never let you fail because you're injured and can't work. Especially since the injury wasn't even your fault." Her expression turned hard. "Do the police have any leads yet?"

"Not many. A security camera caught the license plate. The car was stolen. They haven't found it yet." Mom told me that. She talked to Detective Fiore the same day I had my surgery. She said he was just as frustrated as the rest of us.

Scarlett's mouth twisted. "That's a bummer."

"Yep." I turned my head to stare out the window. I had my doubts if they'd ever find the person who nearly ran us over. Though part of me wondered if it was connected to Phil and Felicity's murders. Daphne said the driver looked right at us. Which meant the woman knew what she was doing. I couldn't think of another reason someone would want to hurt any of us. Unless it was just a random thing. That seemed as unlikely as someone trying to run us over because Darcy and I tried to help the murder victims. We didn't know anything.

Scarlett pulled into the festival grounds at the city park. A guard waved us through, and we bumped over the grass to the spot I'd been assigned. With a little bit of maneuvering, she parked the truck at the correct angle, and we climbed out just as Darcy walked up from where she'd parked.

Together, the three of us worked to get the truck windows open and the power set up. In less than thirty minutes, we had the generator going and the refrigerators were running, keeping the buttercream on my cupcakes from melting. It also powered a fan in the back so we didn't melt, either.

"I'm going to hit up Tyson's truck and see if he's got any breakfast burritos cooking yet." Darcy pointed over an aisle and to the right.

My stomach growled. "Bring me something if he does." Tyson made amazing breakfast burritos. He made amazing burritos. Period.

"Me too," Scarlett said.

Darcy nodded and walked off.

"That didn't take as long as I thought it would." Scarlett took a folding camp chair from the storage locker just inside the back doors of the truck and opened it.

"It helped that there were three of us, and that I don't have to worry about decorating on-the-fly today. A pared down menu makes things easy."

"Speaking of easy. Here comes something easy on the eyes." She glanced past me and nodded.

I turned and saw Jack approaching.

My eyebrows slammed together, and I spun back to Scarlett. I didn't want to talk to him. Not after our conversation last weekend.

"Whoa." She gave me a wide-eyed look. "What did he do?"

"That pretty face hides a jerk."

She frowned. "What did he say?"

"It wasn't so much what he said, just the way he said it. I'm not a child, but he acted like I was."

Her head bobbed. "Got it. He's hideous and a jerkface and we don't like him."

I chuckled. "Thank you, Scarlett, for always having my back."

"Hey, unicorn sticker and pink scrunchie bonds are forever." She reached for the dark ponytail held in place atop her head with a hot pink scrunchie and tightened it, as if readying herself for battle.

"Ladies. Good morning."

Jerkface Fiore's voice washed over me. I tried to ignore the richness to it that slid through my insides like fine wine.

Glancing at him, I murmured a good morning in return but reached inside the truck for the box of napkins. I didn't know how I'd fill the dispenser one-handed, but the attempt would keep me busy so I didn't have to look at him.

"Delaney, it's good to see you here. I wasn't sure you would be."

"I've got great family and friends. They wouldn't let me miss such a big event." I tugged on the box flaps, and it popped open.

"That's good."

From the corner of my eye, I saw him shift his weight from one foot to the other. "Is there anything else, Detective?" I grabbed a handful of napkins and straightened. "We're a little busy."

A frown tweaked his eyebrows. "Would you like some help?"

Scarlett swooped in and took the napkins from me. "No, thank you. We can manage."

His frown intensified.

I fought back a smile at the cold shoulder Scarlett gave him. She seemed determined he'd get the hint and leave us alone.

"Ah, well, okay. Good. I guess I'll leave you to it then. Delaney, I'm glad to see you doing well."

A touch of shame tightened my chest.

Maybe I'd overreacted.

Possibly.

Just a tad.

Maybe all he'd really been doing was looking out for me. We were dealing with murderers, after all.

"Thank you," I said softly, a bit of my anger leaving. "Would—would you like a cookie to go? On the house."

"Oh." His frown turned confused, then smoothed out as he smiled. "Sure."

I pushed the napkin box aside, avoiding the glare Scarlett aimed at me, and stepped into the truck. "Chocolate chip or frosted sugar cookie?" I called through the window.

"Chocolate chip, please. Though if you have any of those fruit tarts, I'll take one of those, and I'll pay you for it. That was amazing."

"Sorry. No fruit tarts this time." I opened a drawer and used a pair of tongs to pick up a chocolate chip cookie and slide it into a small bag. Turning around and taking a step, I passed it through the window. "Maybe at the next event. Once my arm heals."

"Yeah. Maybe." He took the cookie. "Thanks."

I smiled, a little more genuinely than before. "You're welcome."

With a small wave, he walked away.

A shadow fell over the door. I turned to see Scarlett scowling.

"What? Don't look at me like that." I knew she'd be confused. I was confused.

"What happened to, 'He's a jerkface, and we don't like him?'"

I sighed and leaned back against the counter. "He's not hideous." I held up a hand, stopping her from telling me that just because someone was good-looking didn't automatically make them a good person. "And I might have overreacted a bit to what he said. He's a cop, and this is a serious crime. I think—I think, maybe, he just doesn't want me to get hurt." I raised my arm. "Again."

Scarlett stepped inside the truck. "Girl, mark my words. One day, you're gonna marry that man."

A surprised laugh bubbled free. "What? You're crazy. How did you come to that conclusion?"

"You're wishy-washy. We like him, we hate him, we like him again. Pick one!" She held up a finger.

I laughed again. "Trust me, I wish I could." It would make my life easier if I could settle on a single emotion regarding Jack Fiore. I doubted that would ever be the case, though.

Scarlett's exasperation faded and she smiled. "I think you're destined to be confused about him for a long, long time."

Twenty-Six

"We need lunch."

I glanced at Scarlett from where I stood, combining chocolate chip cookies from one tray to another. "Didn't we just have breakfast?" Tyson had in fact been cooking when Darcy went to his truck earlier. I'd eaten a scrumptious egg, hash brown, chorizo, and avocado burrito.

"That was, like, five hours ago, Delaney."

I lifted my left arm to look at my watch, only to realize I didn't have it on because of the cast.

"It's almost one," she said.

"Is it really?" My brow furrowed with surprise. It didn't feel that late. We'd been busy, and the morning had flown past.

She chuckled. "Yes. I think you need a break. How about you run and get us food? I'll man the truck."

"Are you sure?" I removed the empty tray and set it at my feet so I could move the full tray up.

"Yes. Go walk around. Bring me whatever. I just want to eat."

I moved the full trays up, then replaced the empty at the

bottom. "Fine. But don't complain when I bring you back a burger and you wanted noodles."

"I won't. I'd be happy with sauerkraut and sausage right now." She laid a hand over her belly. "My stomach feels like it wants to crawl its way out and eat by itself."

My nose wrinkled. "Thank you for that visual."

She grinned broadly. "You're welcome."

Chuckling softly, I closed the cabinet and removed my apron. After hanging it on a hook on the wall, I picked up my purse and slung it over my neck and one shoulder. "I'll be back."

"Don't rush. But don't take too long, either." She patted her tummy again.

Laughing, I stepped out the door. "Eat a cookie."

"I might eat two!" she called after me.

Outside, I took a quick stock of the festival grounds, then turned left. Wandering down the aisle, I catalogued all the trucks and what they offered. Many of them I knew from other rallies and events.

I waved to a few people and exchanged pleasantries while I walked through the rows, trying to decide on what sounded the best for lunch.

My phone vibrated in my pocket, interrupting my search.

I pulled it out and glanced at the screen.

Uh-oh. It was Scarlett.

Answering, I put it to my ear. "Hey, everything okay?"

"Yeah. Can you do me a favor? I forgot I told Marta Cressley I would bring the items she bought online from the boutique with me today. Can you run downtown and get them?"

Marta Cressley ran a soup and subs food truck. Glancing back, I spotted her. I'd just walked past.

"Sure." Downtown was only a couple of blocks away from the festival grounds at the local park. "Is it marked, so I know what to grab?"

"Yeah. I bagged it all up, and it has the slip sticking out the top with her name on it. I just forgot to grab it last night when I went home."

"This delays your lunch, you know. I was about to make a decision."

She laughed. "It's fine. I'll eat a cupcake."

I huffed. "I'm gonna start charging you."

Her laugh grew louder. "No you won't, because you're not paying me to work."

"True." I sighed, but a smile broke out on my face. "Fine."

"Thanks, Laney. See you in a bit."

"Yep. Bye." I hung up and pocketed my phone.

I guess I was going on a walk.

Turning around, I cut through the row and toward the rides. Weaving through the crowd, I made it to the edge of the park in about five minutes. From there, I followed the sidewalk the two blocks to Scarlett's shop, The Whispering Fern Boutique.

As I reached the store, I glanced in the window, a smile coming to my face. Scarlett had such an eye for design. She took the pieces she ordered from her suppliers or those she found shopping at estate sales and used them not just on mannequins, but as pieces of art. They enhanced the antique armoire she had in the front window, inviting people to come inside and see what treasures they could find to make their closets look as good.

The bell over the door tinkled as I entered.

Ella Kerns, the woman working the shop today, glanced up from her spot behind the counter and smiled. "Delaney, hi. How's the arm?" She tucked a lock of her blonde hair behind her ear.

"Oh, it's healing, I guess. Plated together, so not technically broken anymore."

The young woman wrinkled her nose. "I suppose that's a

good thing, but it doesn't sound pleasant. I'm surprised you're so mobile. I'd be parked on my couch yet."

"No rest for the weary," I said with a soft chuckle. "Scarlett sent me here to pick up a package for Marta Cressley."

"Oh, right. It's in the back. Let me go get it for you. Just a second." Ella walked out from behind the counter and threaded her way through the displays to the employee door at the back of the shop.

As she disappeared, I glanced around. The store was a mix of vintage and new, but it all blended so well together it was hard to tell what was fresh off the sewing machine and what had been passed around for decades. There were several new vintage pieces as well as a new line of summery stuff. I hadn't been in here in a few weeks, so it didn't surprise me Scarlett had changed things up. I'd been too busy to shop. But she had some cute things.

Like that sundress.

My gaze locked onto a gauzy, white, knee-length dress on the rack to my left. I walked over, touching the soft fabric as I examined the small pale pink and green flowers dotting it. Delicate alabaster buttons lined the front of the dress, which had a fitted bodice and wide shoulder straps.

I flicked through the hangars, searching for my size. This was coming home with me.

"It's done, James. Just drop it!"

My hand stalled mid-air, the dress dangling, at the sound of a woman's raised voice in the rear of the store. It sounded familiar.

"Something fishy is going on. I *will* find out what," the man said.

I inched closer. I didn't recognize his voice.

The woman spoke again, but I couldn't hear what she said. They were tucked behind a blanket display.

Changing direction, I moved to a rack full of flowy

blouses and glanced over, now having a line of sight to the couple.

Brown hair cascaded down a woman's back. In front of her, a tall man who appeared to be in his late twenties glowered at her. Dark brows dipped low over his eyes. I watched him rake a hand through his wavy brown hair. His t-shirt bunched up on his bicep.

Was he a tourist? I didn't recognize him, and I knew most of the men in town my age. And I would remember a man my age who looked like him. Any straight, single woman would. He was quite handsome.

"Here you go, Delaney."

The man looked up and the woman turned around. My eyes rounded with surprise.

It was Skyler Brunswick-Taft.

The man's identity clicked. She'd called him James. This was Phil's son.

What could they be arguing about? Phil's estate?

But what about his estate? James was supposed to inherit it all, except what went to Felicity. But with her dead, did that mean he'd get it all?

Averting my gaze, I turned to Ella. She held out a brown paper sack with a paper sticking out that had Marta's name scrawled on it in Scarlett's handwriting.

I tucked the sundress under my casted arm and took the bag. "Thanks." I forced a smile and tried not to stare as James stormed out.

Skyler moved toward the register, a blouse and a scarf in her hands.

"Excuse me." Ella moved toward the counter. I nodded and waited for her to pass, then stepped over to a display of shorts, pretending to look through them until Skyler paid for her items and left.

Before the bell finished tinkling as she exited, I was on the move. Hurrying toward the register, I held up the dress. "Can you put this in the back for me? I didn't bring my wallet." I had cash in my pocket, but not enough to cover it. Besides, I wanted to follow Skyler and see where she went after her argument with James.

"Sure." Ella took the dress.

"Thanks. I'll be back later or tomorrow to pay for it." With a wave of my fingers, I hurried out the door.

On the sidewalk, I glanced to the right, which was the way Skyler turned when she left the boutique. She was a few doors down, her phone in her hand.

I tried not to let my feet slap the concrete as I speed-walked to catch up to her.

She lifted her phone to her ear, then turned into the alley.

I broke into a trot. When I reached the end of the row of shops, I hugged the wall and peered around the brick.

Skyler had her back to me.

"… problem, Nile."

Nile? As in Phil's business partner?

I strained to hear more, wishing I could walk down the alley. But there was nowhere for me to hide if she turned around.

Luckily, the buildings amplified her voice. So long as she didn't walk too much further away, I could hear her from where I was.

"James is suspicious about the real estate transactions. He's determined to get to the bottom of things." She paused, crossing one arm over her waist. Her bag from The Whispering Fern dangled from her fingers. "Oh, you'll take care of it, huh? The way you took care of—" she broke off.

A fierce frown pulled my eyebrows down. Took care of what?

I resisted the urge to growl in frustration. Was Nile responsible for Phil's death? And Felicity's? What reason could he have to kill either of them? That real estate transaction? For what property?

Letting out a huff, I forced myself to continue listening. I had so many questions.

"No, I don't know where he went. Find him yourself. I'm done." Skyler pulled the phone away from her ear and stabbed at the screen with her thumb. She ran a hand through her hair.

I inched back. The last thing I needed was for her to spot me. Questions about what I was doing weren't ones I wanted to answer.

Skyler shifted, turning slightly toward the end of the alley. I shrank back even further.

A moment later, she thrust her phone into her purse and whirled, marching back the way she came.

I ducked out of sight, spinning around and hurriedly walking into the entryway of the print shop on the corner. When she cleared the alleyway and turned right, continuing in the direction she'd started, I moved back onto the main sidewalk and watched her leave.

All the questions I had continued to whirl through my mind. But my thoughts stuck on one as Skyler's final words echoed through my head.

Where was James?

urrying back to The Whispering Fern, I ducked inside.

Ella glanced up and smiled. "Hey, are you back with your wallet?"

"No, I have a question. The man that left just before me, did you see which way he went?"

A frown formed on her pretty face. "Um, left, I think."

"Okay, thanks." Tossing her a smile and a quick wave, I reversed direction and went left. Where could he have gone? Home?

But where was that? He didn't live with Phil.

A thought struck me. With Phil and Felicity both dead, the property likely passed to James. Maybe he was staying there while he was in town. Could he do that?

I wasn't sure, but it seemed plausible.

So, that left me in a bit of a dilemma. Did I go over there? Maybe warn him about what I'd overheard?

Jack's voice, telling me to stay out of things, shouted inside my head.

I rolled my eyes and sighed. He was probably right. I didn't need to get involved.

Fishing my phone out of my pocket, I opened my recent calls. I'd just call him and let him handle it.

I found his number and tapped the screen. The call connected, and I waited for him to pick up.

Except he didn't. It rang six times, then went to voicemail. I let out a huff and listened to his greeting.

"Jack, it's Delaney. I overheard some things between Skyler Brunswick-Taft and Phil's son. I think—I think maybe Nile is involved in all this, and I think James might be in danger. Anyway, I'm not sure where he went. Maybe Phil's house. But, um, yeah. I just wanted to let you know that. Okay, bye." I hung up, then blew out a breath. That hadn't sounded awkward *at all*.

I rolled my eyes and stuffed my phone back into my pocket. Glancing up and down the street, I hoped I'd see James walk out of a store.

But no one who looked anything like James was in sight.

I nibbled on the corner of my mouth, debating what to do.

I shouldn't.

Right?

Right.

I shook my head. It was a dumb idea. What was I supposed to say if I showed up at the house and he was there? This was assuming he actually let me into the neighborhood.

And there was also the issue of how I was supposed to get there.

A car tooted its horn. I glanced toward the street and saw Morgan pull up to the curb beside me.

He rolled the window down and dipped his head to see me. "Hey. What are you doing downtown? Shouldn't you be at the park?"

"Scarlett sent me on a food run, then to pick up something from her store. Where are you headed?" He wasn't dressed for work.

"Home. I had lunch at the festival with Daphne."

"So, you're not busy?" I shouldn't. I really, *really*, shouldn't. But I couldn't shake the feeling James was in danger. If Jack had answered his phone, I'd feel a little better about things. But who knew when he would check his messages?

"No." He drew out the word, his friendly smile turning into a curious frown. "Why?"

"Can you give me a ride?"

"Sure." He popped the locks. "Get in."

I put the bag in the backseat, then got in beside him.

"You're near the playground, right?"

"Actually, I don't want to go back to the park." I pulled the seat belt across my chest and buckled it.

His brow furrowed. "You don't? Where do you want to go?"

My mouth worked, and I sent him a side-eyed glance. "Phil Brunswick's house."

Morgan's frown deepened. "Why?" His dark tone matched his expression.

"I think James is there, and I think he's in danger."

"Okay. So, let's call the police. They're the ones who should handle this. And why do you think he's in danger?"

"I called Jack, but he didn't answer. And I don't have proof of anything. It's just… a… a feeling, okay?"

Words tumbling over themselves, I explained. "I overheard James and Skyler—Phil's sister—arguing in Scarlett's store. He stormed out, then I followed Skyler, and I heard her on the phone with Nile. She said James was a problem, paused, then said, 'Oh, you'll take care of it, huh? The way you took care of —'. He must have cut her off, because she didn't continue. Just told him to find James himself and that she was done."

He blinked, his frown deepening. "And because of that, you think Nile is the one who killed Phil?" His eyebrows rose.

"Delaney, you realize that's crazy, right? Nile wouldn't hurt anyone."

I threw up my hand and let it flop back to my lap. "No, I don't know. How should I? Nile and I don't exactly run in the same circles. And you didn't hear the way Skyler talked." I aimed a finger at him. "Something's going on."

He sighed and pinched the bridge of his nose. "I get that you think that, but—"

I unfastened my seat belt. "Never mind. I'll find another way there." I yanked on the door handle, swinging my leg out to exit the car. I might have thrown a Hail Mary when I asked him to take me to Phil's, but now that I'd stated my theory out loud, I was more sure than ever that James could end up like his father and stepmother.

"Wait." Morgan laid a hand on my shoulder.

I glanced back.

His dark eyes met mine. "You're sure he's in danger?"

Victory surged through my veins. Maybe I wouldn't need a new way to get there. "I can't say for certain, but I do think so, yes."

Chewing on the corner of his mouth, he studied me for several long seconds.

I barely breathed, hoping he'd say yes.

Finally, he looked away and lightly smacked the top of the steering wheel with the flat of his hand. "Fine. Close the door and buckle up."

I pulled my leg in and did as he said.

"Do you have a plan once we get there? Or even how we'll get through the front gates?"

Lifting a hand, I chewed on my nail and cast another side-eyed look at him as a plan formed. He wouldn't like it.

Morgan glanced at me as he pulled away from the curb, then did a double-take when he saw my expression. "No. I know that look. It's the same one Daphne uses when she wants me to do something I won't like. So, whatever you're thinking, no."

I dropped my hand, slumping in my seat. "Oh, come on, Morgan. It's a good plan. All I want you to do is ring the house from the gate, and if James answers, tell him you need to look in Phil's office for a file."

He groaned softly. "Yep. I knew I wouldn't like it."

"It's a good plan! That's a legitimate excuse for us to go to the house. Plus, if James argues he'll look for it and bring it to town, you can tell him you can't have him do that because of client confidentiality."

My soon-to-be brother-in-law scrubbed a hand down his face, then through his wavy dark hair. "Oh, I should have just kept driving." He blew out a breath. "Fine. But only because I know you'll try to find another way past the gates and probably end up getting yourself in trouble."

I pressed my lips together and looked out my window, staying silent. He wasn't wrong. One way or another I'd find James.

Leaving downtown, Morgan headed for the mountain road leading to the Brunswicks' exclusive neighborhood. He didn't speak to me for the rest of the drive. Just stared out at the road, a muscle ticking in his jaw.

Internally, I heaved a sigh. He'd never let me live this down. I was going to owe him for a very long time.

Morgan slowed to a stop outside the gate to the neighborhood. Rolling down his window, he pressed the button on the intercom to ring the Brunswicks' house.

We waited thirty long seconds, and I was about to tell Morgan to forget it, that James wasn't here and to just take me back to the park, when a male voice came over the speaker.

"Hello?"

My eyes widened.

Morgan sat a little straighter. "Hi. My name is Morgan

Dean. I work for Brunswick & Flaherty. We're missing a case file, and I was wondering if I could check Phil's office for it."

"Man, I really don't want to be bothered right now. I'll check his desk and bring it to town if I find it."

"I can't have you do that. It's a confidentiality thing. It will only take me a few minutes."

A long pause came over the line. "All right. But make it quick."

"I will, thanks."

Two seconds later, the gates opened. My heart thumped. Now came the hard part. Convincing James he was in danger.

Twenty-Eight

The Brunswicks' house loomed in front of us as Morgan drove up the driveway and parked beneath the portico.

"You have a plan, yes?" Morgan asked as he came around the front of the car.

I shut my door and nodded. "Just get me inside."

Brows drawn down, he walked to the front door and reached for the bell but dropped his hand before pressing it when we caught sight of James through the sidelights, walking toward us. The heavy wooden door swung inward, and he stared at us with some confusion.

Perfect eyebrows over his light hazel eyes dipped to form a vee as he frowned at me. "You're the woman from the store earlier."

I pasted a bright smile on my face. "I am."

"Can we come in?" Morgan asked. "I'll only be a minute."

James stepped back, his gaze still on me. "Sure."

Once we were inside and the door closed behind us, I introduced myself. "I'm Delaney Fowler. You must be Phil's son, James."

I knew the moment my name clicked. "You're the woman who found him. And Felicity."

"Guilty as charged. Again."

His frown deepened. "Why are you here?" His gaze shot to Morgan and narrowed. "Is there really a case file you need to find?"

Expression blank, Morgan shook his head.

"I'm sorry we lied," I broke in. "I just really needed to talk to you, and I wasn't sure you'd let me in if I showed up out of the blue."

"Are you kidding? You tried to save my dad. Of course I'd let you in." He crossed his arms, his frown easing off some. "What do you need to talk to me about?"

"Is your aunt here?" I didn't see her, but it was a big house.

Some of the darkness returned to his expression. "No. I haven't seen her since I came back from town. Why?"

Oh, boy. I sucked in a breath through my nose and steeled myself for his reaction to what I was about to say.

"I think she knows who killed your dad, and I think it was Nile." The words fell from my tongue in a rush.

James blinked twice before his eyes widened. "What? Have you lost your mind?"

"No." I held up a hand. "I know it sounds crazy, but hear me out?"

A muscle in his jaw ticked. "Go on."

"I overheard you at the store. When you said you'd find out what was going on? After you left, I followed Skyler. She called Nile and told him you were a problem. He must have told her he'd take care of you, because she said, 'like you took care of—' and then broke off before stating to whom or to what she was referring. She also told him to find you himself and that she was done. What were you talking about when you said you'd find out what was going on?"

The angry expression on James's face had morphed into one of confusion. By the time I finished, he wore a look of shock.

He dropped his arms and looked over my head to stare out the window at the driveway. "I can't believe she'd do this."

"Wait." Morgan held up a hand. "Is Delaney right? Did your aunt and Nile have something to do with your dad's death?"

James met his gaze. "Maybe." He pulled a breath in through his nose and looked away briefly. "Do you know what I do for a living?"

I glanced at Morgan, and we both shook our heads.

"I develop real estate. About a year ago, Dad asked me what I knew about a tract of land north of the lake. It was really close to federal land and wasn't on the market. Not yet, anyway. It was owned by an elderly couple, and the husband had just died. I wasn't really interested in it."

"Why not?" Morgan asked.

"It was too far from town and the water views to make it worthwhile to build either a resort or a high-end housing community weren't great. Just not enough lakefront footage for the size of the property. I told him that too. He just said okay, and I never heard about it again." His gaze flicked from Morgan, to me, then back again. "The other day, I went into Dad's office to look for some documents I needed for the probate court, and I found a deed to the land. It listed a company I've never heard of—NPS Global—as the owner. Dad was the signatory on the documents."

Morgan propped his hands on his hips. I could see the wheels spinning in his brain. "You're sure it was for the same tract of land?"

James nodded. "He gave me the specs for it when he asked me about it. The coordinates and boundary lines were the same."

"Did you look up the company?" Morgan continued.

"Yes. It took some digging, but I found out it was set up

under Dad's law practice as a shell. Skyler caught me looking into it, and she got—antsy."

"Antsy?" I raised an eyebrow.

"Yeah. Her face pinched, and she started wringing her hands together as I explained what I was doing. It made me wonder why so I, um—" He stopped and scratched at his temple with one finger, looking a little sheepish. "I might have contacted a friend who has some… special skills, shall we say?"

A hacker. That's what he was getting at without saying it out loud, I surmised. "And this friend found out she was involved?"

"He did, yeah. Dad, Nile, and Skyler bought the land together."

"Why?" Morgan asked. "Not just why did they buy it, but why keep it a secret?"

"That's the part I don't know. Skyler won't talk about it. Just tells me they did it and to drop it."

"We did it for money. Lots and lots of money."

I jumped at the male voice, and the three of us turned toward the hall coming off the kitchen.

"Nile?" James shifted, fully facing the man. "How did you get in? What are you even doing here?"

His steel-blue gaze stayed fixed on James as he reached behind his back. When he brought his hand around, he held a matte-black pistol aimed at James's chest.

"Taking care of a problem."

Twenty-Nine

I edged closer to Morgan. My heart thumped against my ribcage, sending a throbbing through my recently repaired arm.

"Nile, what are you doing?" Morgan took a step forward.

Nile swung the gun toward him. "Stop right there."

Morgan held up his hands and his eyes grew round. "We don't want any trouble, Nile."

He scoffed. "You wouldn't be here asking questions if you truly wanted to stay out of it." His gaze flicked to me. "I guess it's fortunate you can't. You, Ms. Fowler, have been a thorn in my side for the past two weeks. No one would have found Phil for days if not for you. And Felicity would be at the bottom of the lake."

Me and my dumb luck.

"But now I have the opportunity to take care of my biggest problem"—he glanced at James—"and to silence the person who can't keep her nose out of other people's business."

Indignation brought my chin up. "It's my business when people keep dying in front of me." I aimed a glare at Nile as anger flared to life in my chest. This guy killed two people and had the audacity to call me a problem?

"Laney," Morgan hissed.

I ignored him, riled up now. "You really think taking us out will help you get away with what you've done? Detective Fiore knows where we are." That was a lie, but Nile didn't know that. I'd mentioned where I thought *James* was, but not that *I* had gone to find him. "He's probably on his way here now." That wasn't a lie. I hoped. If Jack had checked his messages, he could be on his way to talk to James.

Nile's spine went rigid, and his gaze darted to the front door. "No. No, that won't do." He motioned us toward the kitchen. "Let's go."

"Where?" James asked, his own glare fixed on Nile as he refused to move.

"Away from here." He motioned to the kitchen again. "Go."

James stared hard at him for several seconds. "Dad trusted you. Why would you kill him?"

"I'm not answering anymore questions." He readjusted his grip on the gun. "Get moving or that detective is going to find you here dead on the floor."

Muscles worked in James's jaw, but he took a step forward.

I glanced at Morgan, then we followed.

Nile took out his phone, walking backward to keep an eye on all of us. We moved toward the short hall that ran through the pantry and into a mudroom connected to the garage.

"Change of plans. The cops are closing in," Nile said quietly into the phone. He paused, glancing at me. "Ms. Fowler is proving to be as much of a problem as James." Again, he paused, then nodded. "We're on our way."

My mind spun. Who was he talking to? Skyler? And where was he taking us? What did he—they—plan to do once we got there?

I chewed on the inside of my cheek, desperately trying to come up with a way to escape. If he was any kind of good bad guy, he'd make us ditch our phones. Mine was in my back pocket. Nile hadn't seen it, because the hem of my t-shirt hung down over it.

As we passed through the mudroom and into the garage, I moved directly behind Morgan, using his bigger frame as a shield. With deft fingers, I slid the phone from my pocket, then palmed it and cradled my broken arm. I flicked it to silent with my thumb and slid it into the sling, between my arm and my body.

James opened the door to the garage and stepped in.

Nile ushered Morgan and me through. "That way." He pointed to the door on the back side of the garage that led into the yard.

Skirting the gleaming high-end cars in the garage, we exited the building. The driveway swept out and around disappearing into the trees. From here, I didn't see any vehicles, but that didn't mean Nile wasn't parked behind Morgan.

I doubted it, though. We'd have seen him pull up through the windows around the front door.

"Where are we going?" I asked.

"My guess is the woods, right?" James sent a disparaging look at Nile. "There's a set of trails back there wide enough for a vehicle, and I'm guessing you parked there and walked in." James nodded toward the trees.

"You would be right. But before we go any further, throw your phones into the grass."

Muscles ticked in James's jaw again. A similar set pulsed in Morgan's. Neither man moved to toss their phones.

Nile heaved a heavy breath. He raised the gun and pointed it at me but kept his gaze on James. "How about I shoot her instead of you?"

James's lips turned white as he flattened his mouth into a thin line. With his hazel eyes the color of flint, he plucked his phone from his pocket and dropped it into the grass. "Happy?"

"Yes." Nile turned to Morgan. "Now it's your turn." His gaze dropped to me. "You, too, Ms. Fowler."

"I left my phone in the car." To demonstrate, I lifted the hem of my shirt and turned so he could see all my pockets.

Nile nodded and looked at Morgan. "That just leaves you, Morgan."

Running his tongue over his teeth, anger turned the angled planes of Morgan's handsome face even harder. He stuck a hand in his back pocket and pulled out his phone. It landed on the ground near James's.

"Thank you, gentlemen. We can proceed now." He motioned us toward the tree line.

We walked in a staggered single file into the pine forest. Soon, the thick branches obscured our view of the house.

A hundred yards in, the undergrowth thinned, and we turned onto a path just wide enough for a vehicle. I scanned the forest, hoping to see another person out walking. Just someone I could call out to for help.

But there was no one. Birds and squirrels in the thick ferns and pine boughs were the only creatures stirring.

Five minutes later, a vehicle came into view. My heart kicked into double-time, thinking—hoping—we'd come across someone, but we had not. It was Nile's car.

The vehicle beeped twice when he unlocked it.

"Ms. Fowler, Morgan, in the back, please. James, you can sit up front with me."

We got in the car as requested. I made sure to sit behind Nile so he couldn't look back and see my hands. If I could, I planned to text Jack.

I glanced around the dim interior of the car. But not until we made it out of the forest and into the sunshine. In the shaded forest, my phone screen would light up the vehicle like a Christmas tree.

Nile started the car and put it in gear. We bumped down the path, rocking and rolling over the uneven ground.

I gritted my teeth. With every jolt, pain shot through my arm. I'd thought I'd done a good job staying on top of the pain since my surgery. Yesterday, I'd only taken the stronger painkiller when I went to bed. It had only ached a little this morning, so I just took ibuprofen. Now I wished I had the stronger stuff.

A particularly deep rut sent me crashing into the door. I let out a soft cry as my arm collided with the window.

"Watch it," Morgan growled at Nile. "No one knows we're back here, so slow down."

Nile rolled his eyes. "You think I care if she bashes her arm a time or two? She'll be dead soon, anyway, so it isn't like it will matter."

Fear stabbed me in the chest, quickening my pulse and making sweat bead on my brow. I swallowed and tamped it down, grasping onto the sliver of anger that also flared to life at his words. I'd survived nearly being run over by a car and went through surgery to repair the damage. This bottom-dweller wouldn't take me out now. I refused to die after all of that.

So, I bided my time, hooking my good arm through Morgan's to keep from hitting the door again.

Eventually, he turned onto the main road in the neighbor-hood, then left through the front gates. I stared at the tall iron frame as we passed through. Phil must have given him the code in the past to get in. Or he lived in the neighborhood. I honestly didn't know where he lived.

Outside the gates, he turned right. Once I was sure he was paying more attention to the road and to James beside him, I slid my phone from my sling. Holding it down between my knees to keep it out of sight, I cast a furtive look at it as I opened the messaging app to text Jack.

Help! I typed, then hit send.

I tapped the message bar again and wrote out another quick text.

Nile did it. In his car on Sadler Mtn Rd heading away from town.

Hitting send again, I kept the phone in my hand, waiting for the telltale buzz that he'd replied.

I didn't have to wait long.

With a quick check up front to make sure Nile still wasn't paying attention to me, I glanced at the screen.

On my way. Do what he says until I find you.

Not a problem. Now that I knew the cavalry was coming, I was perfectly fine playing the good girl.

K, I typed, then tapped send. With the message sent, I turned off the screen and slipped the device back into my sling. Glancing at Morgan, I gave him a quick nod. He'd been watching me.

I turned to look out the window.

Now we just had to wait. Something I wasn't particularly good at.

For the next several minutes, I kept one eye on the road ahead and another on the rearview mirror, watching for a vehicle to come up behind us.

But the road stayed frustratingly empty in both directions.

It didn't take me long to realize, though, that Nile was looping around the lake. But to where, I didn't know. Possibly to the property he'd bought with Phil and Skyler. This side was less developed due to a poorer road network and less lake frontage. James was right. People didn't want to live up here because it didn't have the views other areas of the lake did.

We turned off the main road—which wasn't much more than a paved track through the woods—and onto a dirt road leading down toward the lake.

Nile hit a hole, and my butt left the seat. I clenched my teeth, hanging onto Morgan with a death-grip again as we rocked and rolled over deep potholes, washboard ridges, and several melon-size rocks embedded in the ground. This road was in worse shape than the path through the Brunswicks' neighborhood.

After several minutes of bumping over the ground, the trees parted, and the lake came into view. If the situation weren't so dire, I'd admire the sight before me. Sunlight glittered off the narrow strip of glassy water in sight. A couple of boats dotted the surface, one leaving a white trail in its wake. An eagle soared overhead, swooping low to scan the lake for its next meal before changing course to sail high once more.

At the shoreline, a boat waited. It looked much like Coral Peabody's *Night Dragon* but had less black and gray and more white and gold. From this vantage point, I couldn't see the name.

"Everybody out." Nile parked and shut the car off, lifting the gun from his lap, pointing it at James.

Reaching across my body, I pulled on the door handle and got out. I looked over my shoulder, up the road we'd just come down, hoping to see Jack barreling toward us.

But only pine boughs moved.

"Let's go. Down to the boat."

I grimaced. I did not want to do that, but I didn't see that I had much choice.

"Whose boat is this?" Morgan asked.

"A friend's," Nile answered.

That didn't help me. If I wanted to relay information to Jack, I needed some specifics.

Nile ushered us down the embankment and onto a short dock.

I said a quick prayer of thanks when we stepped onto the planks. The boat's name was visible.

Marilyn Mon-row.

I held back a snort. Original.

Reaching the stern, Nile banged on the hull. "We're here!"

A sharp frown creased my forehead. I shot a look at Morgan and James. Could Skyler have made it all the way here before us? But where was her car? Nile's was the only one around.

The rear cabin door opened.

Morgan gasped.

Thirty

"Mandi?" The incredulity in Morgan's voice matched the surprise pinging through my mind.

The woman stepped fully onto the deck and sent him a sunny smile that didn't reach her cold eyes.

This was the law office's secretary? Where was the quiet, slightly flighty woman I'd met the day Phil died?

"Hi, Morgan. I'm surprised to see you here, but also not." Her gaze flicked to me. "The company you keep leaves something to be desired."

I narrowed my eyes at the slight.

"How are you involved?" Morgan asked.

She raised her eyebrows. "You really think Phil and Nile are bright enough to come up with this scheme on their own? I've been the driving force in that law firm since the day Nile hired me. I've brought in new clients and made sure old ones stayed happy all while playing the ditzy secretary role." She grinned, flashing bright white teeth at him. "I could have had a great career in Hollywood, but figured getting this one and his partner to reward me handsomely for using the same talent was a lot easier." She nodded to Nile. "Plus, they like the benefits." Aiming a sultry look at

Nile, she adjusted the neckline of her sleeveless button-up blouse downward.

"They're very nice benefits, yes," Nile agreed with a wolfish grin.

"What scheme?" James cut in. "Are you talking about the real estate deal?" He glanced around. "This is the property, isn't it? What's so special about it? Why the secrecy?"

Mandi shrugged. "The land itself isn't much of a prize. Too isolated. But"—she wagged a finger—"that's also what makes it so great." She motioned them forward. "Come aboard. We need to move."

Nile poked James in the arm with his pistol.

Giving the older man a glare, James hopped on board. Morgan went next, helping me climb on. Nile brought up the rear, bringing the mooring lines with him. Mandi led us inside and to the bridge.

"Have a seat." She pointed to the bench lining the rear wall.

I didn't like the idea of sitting—it was an extra step to stand up and get away—but Jack's plea to do as told echoed through my mind.

Live to fight later, Laney, I told myself.

Nile moved to the helm, joining Mandi, but kept his weapon trained in our direction as he spoke to her. "Did you talk to Contreras and tell him to cease operations for now?"

"Yes. He's clearing the last of the crew out now."

"What crew?" James asked. "Someone please explain what's going on and why you killed my father." He planted his feet and crossed his arms.

Mandi sighed. "I would tell Nile to shoot you here and drop your body over the side, but we're too close to shore." She wrinkled her nose and glared at me. "Not that it made a difference with Felicity."

Suddenly, it all clicked in my brain. "You killed her, didn't you? And made it look like Gage did it. And you're the one who tried to run me and my sisters down last week." Daphne had seen a blonde woman behind the wheel. Before seeing Mandi, if given a chance to think about it, I would have thought it was Skyler behind the wheel, wearing a blonde wig. But cold, calculating Mandi Davis made much more sense.

"Guilty." Her smile turned sickly sweet, then dropped away. "You were asking too many questions, getting too nosy. Especially since you're so buddy-buddy with that cop." She rolled her eyes. "Why Sheriff Driemeyer had to suddenly develop principles and hire a *real* detective is beyond me." She blew out a quick breath. "But what's done is done. Now we just have to avoid him."

Nile handed her his gun, then started the engines. A rumble vibrated through my hips and up my spine.

James half-rose from his seat, fists balled at his sides. "Tell me why you killed him. Or you can just kill me here and take your chances with the detective."

Tipping her nose up, she gave him a disdainful look. "He grew a conscience, that's why."

"Over what?"

"Murder." Once again, she rolled her eyes. "See, there is some prime timber on federal land just up that way." She pointed up the mountain. "This property"—she pointed down—"is isolated and vast, and there's no fence. We can just walk loggers right over the boundary line. With the area's ranger position currently unfilled, there is no one around to stumble over us. Someone only comes from the next district over once a month, and they don't do much more than take a quick drive and talk to the sheriff to make sure there's nothing crazy going on. Driemeyer doesn't like the feds, so he's happy to say, 'Nope. Everything's good,' and move on."

Mandi propped her hands on her hips, her eyes on James. "But then your father had to go and get himself into a bit of a divorce pickle. Felicity wanted his assets reexamined, claiming he had some that were undeclared."

Another thing clicked in my brain. "The file she brought him at work the day you killed him. It contained papers pertaining to this property, didn't it?"

Mandi clucked her tongue. "You're smarter than I give you credit for. But she didn't 'find' it," she said, making air quotes with one hand. "Phil could be careless with case files and other paperwork. I was forever picking up and putting away files he left in the boardroom. But in this instance, she overheard him and Skyler talking about the property and went in search of the contracts. She broke into his desk and found the file. What she brought to the office was a copy. She told him she was taking it to her attorney."

"Wait. Detective Fiore told me he knew what was in the file Felicity brought that day. Why hasn't he figured this out already?" Jack was far from dumb. Digging into NPS Global —the company on the papers—would have been the first thing he did.

Nile snorted. "You don't think I gave him the *actual* file she brought, do you?" He rolled his eyes.

I narrowed mine and glared. He didn't have to be condescending about it.

James frowned and spoke before I could reply. "I don't understand. It's not a crime to own property. What you wanted to do, yes, but she didn't know about that. Did she?"

"No," Nile said. "But she risked exposing our operation. Bringing the property into the divorce proceedings would have added undue scrutiny. Something we didn't need."

I looked at Morgan. A slight wrinkle to his forehead showed his confusion. I had a feeling he was thinking the same thing I was. Why kill Phil?

James must have had the same thought, because he voiced the question. "Why not eliminate Felicity, then? Why Dad?"

"Because your father wasn't a murderer." Mandi's tone

was matter-of-fact. "Neither is your aunt, but she wisely decided to keep her mouth shut. Phil, though, couldn't stomach the idea of murdering anyone and threatened to go to the police with our plan to silence your stepmother. We couldn't have that."

Nile pushed the throttle higher, maneuvering the boat away from the dock.

"So, what do you plan to do with us?"

Mandi's mirthless smile returned. "You'll meet your end the way Felicity should have. But this time, I'll make sure you reach the bottom of the lake."

The fear I'd pushed out earlier made a return, but this time, I couldn't make it go away again. No one knew where we were. I couldn't text Jack and tell him while Mandi continued to hover. There was no hiding behind Morgan or the seat here. I was in plain view.

Leaning back, I closed my eyes. A single tear leaked out as I said a silent prayer for strength. And for a plan.

Resolve filled me.

I refused to die like this. Refused to let Mandi and Nile win.

When Mandi looked away, I leaned into Morgan. "We need a plan."

"Yeah. You think you can fake an argument with me?"

I sent him a sly look, then sat back.

Could I fake an argument? I resisted the urge to roll my eyes. I'd been the lead in every school play all four years of high school. And I was the middle child. Drama and chaos were in my blood.

I didn't waste any time coming up with something.

"What do you mean you're glad Daphne's not like me?" I said, turning an angry frown on him. "She's very much like me. Who do you think it was who ignored the staff-only sign and snuck into the back of Coral Peabody's gallery?" In fact, it had been Darcy, but that little detail didn't matter right now.

"She would *not* do that," he shot back, running with it.

"I guess you don't know her as well as you think you do." I crossed my good arm over the bad one and tipped my nose into the air.

"Or maybe you're just a liar who needs to be the center of attention all the time." He turned in his seat to face me.

I looked at him, blinking in surprise at the hard set to his face. If it weren't for the softness in his eyes, I'd think he was serious.

"That's what this is, isn't it? Why you've been so hell bent on sticking your nose into Detective Fiore's investigation? You're jealous Daphne's getting attention because we got engaged. You want the focus back on yourself."

I scoffed and rolled my eyes at him. "That is such a load of crap."

"Whatever. I can't wait until Daphne and I are married and can move away from here."

I sent him a sharp look. He had better not be serious about moving away.

"I won't have to put up with you or Darcy, and I especially won't have to put up with your parents." He sneered and crossed his arms. "Your mother could try the Pope's patience."

I wanted to laugh, because he wasn't wrong on that, but we weren't going for funny. We were going for angry.

So, I shot to my feet and stabbed a finger at him. "You take that back!"

He rose, too, and stood toe-to-toe with me. "No. It's the truth. She's pushy, opinionated, bossy—all the things that make a woman unlikeable. How she raised someone so soft-spoken and demure as Daphne is beyond me."

I pressed my lips together to hold back the laugh. Daphne was demure. And she could be soft-spoken. But she was also opinionated and bossy. Two qualities I knew for a fact Morgan appreciated in his fiancée. She wouldn't hesitate to push me or Darcy into doing something.

"Hey!" Mandi walked closer. "Sit down and shut up. You can have your little family squabble somewhere else."

Whipping my head to the side, I glared at her. "Really? When? At the bottom of the lake? You plan to murder us in just a little while, remember? So, no. I don't think I'll sit down. This has been brewing between us for a while now, so I think we'll have it out. Then I can die with a clear conscience."

Turning back to Morgan, I shoved a finger into the middle of his chest and let my imagination take over, lying through my teeth. "Daphne only chose you because she's afraid of being alone. The guy she really wants married one of her co-workers. She was tired of being sad every time she saw the woman, so you coming along was perfect timing."

His eye twitched. "Liar! She loves me."

I snorted. "You keep telling yourself that." Seizing the moment, I used the fast pace of our argument and the heated emotions to take Mandi and Nile by surprise. If we had any chance of escape, we needed to split up and make them chase us. They only had the one weapon as far as I could tell.

Sticking my nose in the air and giving Morgan a disgusted look, I spun on my heel and flounced off the bridge.

"Hey! Stop!"

Mandi's shout followed me out, but I didn't stop. I rounded the corner, running along the gangway, scrambling through the opening that led to the boat's nose. One-handed, I hopped down the short ladder to the next deck, landing in the outdoor shower area.

The boat slowed abruptly, and I stumbled, banging into the wall. Pain spread through my arm like a fiery poker. I clenched my teeth but kept going, knowing Mandi wouldn't be far behind.

A shot rang out, immediately followed by a metallic ping as the bullet ricocheted off the railing. With a shriek, I ducked but didn't stop moving, making my way around the storage bench to the gangway on the port side. Under the cover of the deck above, I straightened and took off at a sprint. My sneakers squealed on the smooth wood floor as I skidded to a halt in front of the doors leading to the main cabin. Grabbing the door handle, I pushed inside.

Pausing for a second to take stock of the room, I spotted a hallway toward the rear of the room and took off at a run through the luxuriously appointed space, weaving through cream leather couches and gleaming wood tables. My feet made soft thuds on the carpeted floor as I hurried down the hallway. Passing two doors, I turned into a third on my right.

It was a bedroom. And a nice one.

With a really big closet.

I flung the door open and stepped into the wardrobe, shoving aside dresses to hide behind them. Reaching out, I hooked my fingers around the edge of the door and pulled it closed as far as I could. The inside of the panel was smooth, so I couldn't grab hold to fully close it. I just had to hope Mandi wouldn't notice it was slightly ajar.

Fully hidden, I took my phone from my sling and woke up the screen. There were no messages from Jack, but I hadn't really expected any. He probably didn't want to chance drawing attention to the device in case it buzzed.

I found his name in my contacts and tapped it, then brought the phone to my ear.

It rang twice before he answered.

"Delaney? Where are you? I've been up and down Sadler Mountain Road and saw no sign of Nile's car."

"We're on a boat on the north end of the lake," I whispered. "I'm hiding in a closet. Morgan and James Brunswick are with me. I'm sorry. I should have listened to you." Tears gathered in my eyes and several spilled over.

"Just tell me where you are. You can have regrets later."

I sniffed. He was right. Until we were safe, I needed to keep it together. Getting upset would help nothing. "We're on a yacht named *Marilyn Mon-row*." I spelled the second part of the boat's name for him. "I think it's Mandi Davis's yacht."

"Mandi Davis? The secretary?"

"Yeah. She's the mastermind. All of this is over some illegal logging. We turned off onto a dirt road. It led to a dock."

He muttered a curse. "I think I just passed there."

"Don't come this way," I urged, my whisper a little louder than I intended. I forced myself to calm. The last thing I needed was for Mandi to find me. "We're on the lake, but not terribly far from where we launched. You need a boat to get to us."

Jack let out a groan of frustration. "I don't know this area well enough to know where I can find the nearest dock."

I thought about where Nile and Mandi's dock was in relation to my parents' inn. It was on the other side of the lake. Too far for him to reach us quickly.

But Coral Peabody's house was nearby. And it didn't matter that the police probably impounded her yacht. She had other boats. All the million-dollar-plus homes did.

"You let Gage Peabody out of jail, right?" I thought I'd heard the police released him.

"Yes. I didn't have enough to hold him. Why?"

I shifted, peering through the tiny crack for any sign of movement. All seemed quiet. "Go back toward town and knock on his door. He'll gladly let you use a boat or a jet-ski if it means catching Felicity's killer."

He huffed. "Why am I not surprised you know about the two of them?"

"Yves came to see me."

A soft grunt came over the line. "Tell me what's happening on the boat."

"I can't see anything. I'm still in the closet. But Morgan and I staged an argument. We used the chaos as a chance for me to run and hide so I could call you. I think Mandi's the only one with a gun. Though I could be wrong. There might have been another up on the bridge I didn't see. I don't know if Morgan and James are still up there, or even if they're all right. I haven't heard any sounds of fighting or other gun shots than the one Mandi fired at me."

"She shot at you?" His voice rose.

I closed my eyes, hearing the *ping!* of the bullet hitting the rail. My stomach turned. "Yeah." I swallowed around the sudden lump in my throat. "How far away are you?"

"Just a couple minutes to the Peabody's. Do you hear anything yet?"

"No." The word barely escaped.

"Hang in there, Delaney. I'll get there just as fast as I can."

More tears formed in my eyes. I squeezed my eyes shut and felt the moisture trickle out to slide down my cheeks.

I said a prayer he was quick enough.

Thirty-One

I stayed hunkered down in the closet for another five minutes. When Jack reached the Peabody's house and got permission from Gage to use a speedboat, he ended the call.

I knew it was crazy, but I felt safer talking to him. He couldn't do anything to save me if Mandi burst in, but that didn't stop me from feeling like I was less alone with his voice in my ear.

Stowing the phone in my sling once again, I shifted, peering through the small crack in the door to the stateroom.

A soft thump in the hallway froze all the air in my lungs. The door into the room swooshed open with a whisper. I tipped my head, peering through the yards of fabric hanging in my face so I could see out the crack in the door. But the sliver it was open wasn't enough to see who entered, just a faint sense of movement.

It wasn't Jack, that much I knew. Not enough time had passed for him to reach us.

And I figured it wasn't Morgan or James. If they were roaming the boat, I imagined they would call my name.

That left Mandi or Nile.

I parted the dresses keeping me hidden. Silently, I turned

my foot side-to-side, pushing it forward across the wardrobe floor. Leaning toward the door, I strained to hear, hoping to pinpoint where the person was in the room.

A shadow passed in front of the door, then suddenly stopped.

My stomach sank. A surety settled over me that they'd spotted the open closet.

The shadow shifted again, but didn't move away from the door.

My spine stiffened. I couldn't let them find me. I'd be a sitting duck if they opened the door and saw me inside.

I had to do *something*.

Decision made, my muscles tensed.

Oh, man, this was going to hurt.

Using my legs, I drove my body into the door. With a fierce yell born from the desire not to die, I burst through, smacking the wooden panel into the person on the other side.

A feminine grunt of surprise sounded.

It was Mandi.

She fell to the ground, and I landed on top of her. Pain spread through my arm like liquid fire, stealing my breath. But the adrenaline surge kept me going. That and the sight of the gun flying from her hand and tumbling under the bed.

"Get off!" Grabbing my arms, she tried to push me away.

I yanked my good arm free and thrust my open palm into her nose. It glanced off her face, and my momentum carried me across her body. Without the use of my left arm, I couldn't catch myself and faceplanted onto the carpet.

Mandi scrambled to her knees and over me, going for the gun beyond my head under the bed. I pushed up and used my left leg to lash out. I couldn't let her get the weapon.

My foot connected with her side, knocking her back. I rolled and sat up. Before I could get off my butt, she barreled into me.

I landed on my back and all the air rushed from my lungs, leaving me gasping like a fish.

No!

The thought barely cleared my mind when legs ran into my field of vision. Long, tan, hairy ones.

I followed them up.

James.

He moved around me and lifted Mandi off the floor, holding her securely by one arm. "Stop!" He gave her a firm shake. "It's over. You're done."

She blew a lock of blonde hair out of her face, looking up at him. Icicles fairly shot from her eyes. "I should have just hired someone to tamper with the ventilation system at your dad's house. It would have taken care of all my problems, and no one would have been the wiser."

Muscles ticked in James's face and a vein pulsed in his temple. "Well, lucky for us, you wanted a more personal touch." He turned to me. "You okay?"

I sat up, brushing my hair back. "Yeah. I think so." My arm throbbed like the devil, and I wasn't too sure my stitches were still intact, but other than that, I was fine. "I got a hold of Detective Fiore. He's on his way." I slid my hand into my sling and withdrew my phone, sending Mandi a cheeky smile as I gave the phone a little wave.

"Good." He gave Mandi's arm a tug. "Come on. You can join Nile on the aft deck."

As James hauled her out of the room, I rose on shaky legs, following much more slowly. By the time I reached the four of them, I could see a boat speeding toward us, two men at the helm.

I leaned against the wall, waiting for it to arrive. My legs wanted me to sit, but I was afraid I wouldn't want to get back up if I did. So, I stayed where I was.

It took several more minutes for the boat to reach us and

for Jack and Gage to tie up. Sirens echoed over the lake, signaling that more help was on the way.

Jack stepped onto the deck and paused, taking in the scene. He shook his head, disbelief evident in his eyes. "Someone explain."

"Delaney and I staged an argument." Morgan gestured to me. "In the confusion, she took off running. Mandi went after her and that left Nile alone with us." He glanced at James. "Nile tried to pull a gun from the console, but we wrestled it away from him."

"I went after Mandi once we subdued him," James said. "I didn't trust myself to be with him alone." That muscle in his jaw ticked again.

"Which one of you killed Felicity?" Gage, who'd been shifting his weight from foot to foot while he stood just behind Jack, stepped forward. I was surprised Jack let him come, but maybe he hadn't wanted to waste time convincing the man to stay behind.

No one spoke, myself included, though I knew it was Mandi. The red mottling to his face said he was riding a thin line with his temper.

"Who?" He took another step, and Jack grabbed his shirt.

"Gage, I warned you about this before we left."

The man's fists clenched and unclenched. His hard gaze traveled from Nile to Mandi several times before he finally stepped back.

He shook off Jack's hold. "I'll be on my boat." With a quick swish of his shoe on the wooden deck, he walked away.

Jack waited until Gage was out of earshot before he spoke again. "He poses a good question. Who killed her? And Phil?"

"Mandi killed Felicity," I said. The memory of Felicity's pale, lifeless body hanging over my kayak made my stomach churn. "She tried to frame Gage."

Nile spoke up. "She killed Phil too."

"And I should have killed you as well," Mandi shot back.

"Okay, then. Before we go any further, I need to advise you both of your rights." Jack read Mandi and Nile their Miranda rights, then placed them both in cuffs.

I pressed a hand to my belly, willing the butterflies to go away. The adrenaline was wearing off, and it was sinking in just how close I'd come to dying.

But the danger was gone.

Phil and Felicity's killer was in custody.

The healing so many had to do, though, was just beginning.

Thirty-Two

The warm breeze coming off the lake danced over my skin as I sat in a chaise near the beach at the inn. Dappled sunlight came through the trees, kissing my face while my mind drifted. I'd been out here about an hour, dozing on and off.

Once Jack's colleagues arrived on Mandi's yacht, we'd spent some time giving statements, and he'd called a medical team to come check my arm. I had indeed torn out most of my stitches. The police boat had whisked me back to shore, then taken me to the hospital to have them repaired.

Jack had also called my parents to come pick me up.

I wasn't sure how I felt about that. While I was grateful to have their help, I wasn't a kid who needed to be "handled." It was the same attitude that irked me the other day. When I said as much to Mom, she said she didn't think that had been his intention. That she'd heard concern in his voice. She thought he was just worried about me and wanted to make sure I was safe and had what I needed.

I puffed a breath through my nose and shifted, bringing my unencumbered arm up to cross over my abdomen.

Why did he have to invade my solitude? I didn't want to

think about him and his intentions or really anything that didn't bring me unmitigated joy. I'd had enough stress today to last me the rest of the summer.

The soft shuffle of feet through the grass drew me out of my drowsy state.

I kept my eyes closed and settled deeper into the chair. "I'm fine, Mom."

"Glad to hear it."

One eye popped open at the male voice. "You're not my mother."

James smiled down at me. "No. Sorry."

"Don't be. I didn't want to be hovered over." A frown wrinkled my forehead as a thought struck. I opened both eyes. "You're not here to hover, are you?"

He chuckled. "No. May I join you?" He pointed to the second chaise a few feet away.

"Sure."

"Thanks." Moving forward, he folded his long frame and sat down.

I rolled my head to the side to look at him. He held my gaze for several moments, then glanced down at his hands clasped between his knees.

"I, um, wanted to thank you." He looked up, a deep sincerity shining in his hazel eyes. "It means a lot to me that you tried to save my dad. Even though it didn't change the outcome. Felicity too. She wasn't my favorite person, but she didn't deserve what Mandi did to her."

No, she didn't. No one deserved that.

"I also wanted to thank you—and Morgan—for trying to warn me. You could have left it to the police, but you didn't. And having the three of us together made all the difference. I probably wouldn't have been able to escape on my own. That argument you staged with Morgan was something. It almost sounded real."

A smile stretched my lips and crinkled my eyes. "He's like

a brother. Not a word was true." I thought about the things he said about Mom, and my smile widened. "Well, not in the context they were said. My mom is pushy and bossy and opinionated, but not in a negative way."

James returned my smile. He hooked a thumb toward the inn. "I noticed. When I arrived and asked to talk to you, she gave me this mama bear look that dared me to upset you."

"That sounds about right." I chuckled. "So, what happens next for you? Did the police find your aunt?"

He cleared his throat, his brows twitching with a troubled frown. "Yeah. Detective Fiore said they caught up to her in town. She kept shopping, unaware of what Nile and Mandi were up to."

I let out an inelegant snort. Wow. To be that cold-hearted that you could just continue with leisure pursuits without a care was unfathomable to me. "She had me as bamboozled as Mandi. I believed her grief when I spoke to her the day after your dad died."

His head wavered. "I think she grieved, but she was complicit to his murder out of self-preservation. And it's the same with her attitude toward Nile wanting to kill me. If it got out that she was part of an illegal logging scheme—and it was on federal land—it would ruin her."

"It doesn't excuse it, though."

"No. It doesn't." He sat up a bit and ran a hand through his hair. "Anyway, it's going to be a mess untangling Dad's life. I think I'm going to ask Morgan to run the law practice. At least for now."

I frowned. "Isn't Nile still technically in charge?"

"Yes, but I plan to file an injunction on Tuesday and ask the court to grant me temporary control. All of Dad's assets, including his stake in the law firm, are in a trust, and I'm the sole beneficiary now that Felicity's dead. I need someone I can trust to run the firm. I think Morgan's that person."

I looked out over the water and nodded. "He'll have his

hands full. I wonder if Mandi was the only other one involved in criminal activity there?"

"Probably not. There are a few senior staff members who will see some scrutiny from the authorities. The entire practice will. But I trust Morgan to steer the ship through this nightmare."

"Are you staying in Fernwood, then?"

"For now, yes. I can work from anywhere, so I'll set up at Dad's."

I smiled. "Well, good. I hope you stay. Fernwood's a great place."

"Delaney!"

Darcy's voice carried through the air, and we both turned to see her coming down the hill from the inn.

"I'm beginning to see that," James said, his gaze fixed on my sister.

My eyes moved between him and Darcy. A slow, sly smile formed as I took in the intrigued expression on his face.

"What's up?" I asked as Darcy reached us.

"Mom sent me to tell you dinner's ready."

"Oh. Great." My stomach rumbled. I hadn't been hungry until she said something, but now that my brain was aware there was food waiting, it was eager to remind me I hadn't eaten since breakfast. Nile took me captive before I could eat lunch.

Darcy turned to James, her smile turning softer and a little shy. "She told me to invite you to stay."

I rolled my lips inward, then held onto my bottom lip, suppressing a smile. This was interesting. Darcy was never shy.

A smile spread over James's face, crinkling the corners of his eyes. "Really? I could go for a homecooked meal. Is your mother a decent cook?" His gaze encompassed both of us.

I barked a short laugh. "No. But our dad is."

"Oh." He chuckled. "My mistake. Sorry. I just assumed—"

Darcy waved a hand. A teasing smile lit her features. "It's fine. She gets it a lot. She can bake, but cooking is Dad's arena. Come on." She waved us toward the house. "Let's go eat. I'm starving."

"Me too." I swung my legs over the chaise.

James stood. "Here, let me help you." He leaned down and slid an arm under mine to help me to my feet.

"Thank you." Secretly, I was glad he offered his assistance. I wasn't exactly woozy, but today's events and the painkillers I downed earlier had taken their toll. Mostly, I was just tired.

"Did someone go pick up my cat?" Mom and Dad insisted I stay with them tonight. Too tired and too worn out from this past week to argue, my only caveat was that someone bring Millie over so she wasn't alone.

"I did," Darcy said. "She's waiting inside."

The final piece of me relaxed. "Perfect." I pulled away from James and headed for the inn. "Let's go eat."

After spending most of her adulthood moving around the U.S. and Europe, Ashely has settled in her home state of Ohio with her husband, two kids, and a menagerie of pets. She started writing in her teens and never stopped. Her first novel, a romantic thriller under the pen name Ashley A. Quinn, debuted in 2016, and she has since published more than twenty books. When not writing, you can find her with her nose stuck in a mystery thriller or binge-watching British TV dramas and reality shows. She is an avid baseball fan and also enjoys growing all the things in her garden and book-binding.

9 781959 943310